SHUT UP AND KISS ME

LAUREN BLAKELY

ALSO BY LAUREN BLAKELY

Big Rock Series

Big Rock

Mister O

Well Hung

Full Package

Joy Ride

Hard Wood

Happy Endings Series

My Single-Versary

A Wild Card Kiss

Shut Up and Kiss Me

Kismet

Rules of Love Series

The Rules of Friends with Benefits (A Prequel Novella)

The Virgin Rule Book

The Virgin Game Plan

The Virgin Replay

The Virgin Scorecard

Men of Summer Series

Scoring With Him

Winning With Him

All In With Him

The Guys Who Got Away Series

Dear Sexy Ex-Boyfriend

The What If Guy

Thanks for Last Night

The Dream Guy Next Door

The Gift Series

The Engagement Gift

The Virgin Gift

The Decadent Gift

The Extravagant Series

One Night Only

One Exquisite Touch

My One-Week Husband

MM Standalone Novels

A Guy Walks Into My Bar

One Time Only

The Bromance Zone

The Heartbreakers Series

Once Upon a Real Good Time

Once Upon a Sure Thing

Once Upon a Wild Fling

Boyfriend Material

Asking For a Friend

Sex and Other Shiny Objects

One Night Stand-In

Lucky In Love Series

Best Laid Plans

The Feel Good Factor

Nobody Does It Better

Unzipped

Always Satisfied Series

Satisfaction Guaranteed

Instant Gratification

Overnight Service

Never Have I Ever

PS It's Always Been You

Special Delivery

The Sexy Suit Series

Lucky Suit

Birthday Suit

From Paris With Love

Wanderlust

Part-Time Lover

One Love Series

The Sexy One

The Only One

The Hot One

The Knocked Up Plan

Come As You Are

Sports Romance

Most Valuable Playboy

Most Likely to Score

Standalones

Stud Finder

The V Card

The Real Deal

Unbreak My Heart

The Break-Up Album

The Caught Up in Love Series

The Pretending Plot (previously called *Pretending He's Mine*)

The Dating Proposal

The Second Chance Plan (previously called *Caught Up In Us*)

The Private Rehearsal (previously called *Playing With Her Heart*)

Seductive Nights Series

Night After Night

After This Night

One More Night

A Wildly Seductive Night

ABOUT

When a scorching one-night stand between best friends absolutely, definitely shouldn't happen again...

How to resist sleeping with your best friend when you're stuck in a hotel room in Vegas with the charming, glasses-wearing hottie.

1. Slather your face in a grapefruit mask
2. Wear a big, fluffy robe
3. Make him do the same.

Oops.

Didn't work. Turns out our libidos had other plans.

But, no biggie. After epic, soul-shattering banging, I'll just put the genie back in the bottle the next morning. Only, that's easier said than done. After years of scraping by, Nolan and I just landed the big break of a lifetime for our scrappy online restaurant review show. We're going to New York for a month.

Just the two of us. **TOGETHER ALL THE TIME.**

But I've already lost my best friend once, so I'll do whatever it takes to resist thoroughly delicious Nolan again.

Until I learn whatever it takes might cost me everything.

SHUT UP AND KISS ME

A HAPPY ENDINGS NOVEL

By Lauren Blakely

Want to be the first to learn of sales, new releases, preorders and special freebies? Sign up for my VIP mailing list here! You'll also get free books from bestselling authors in a selection curated just for you!

PRO TIP: Add lauren@laurenblakely.com to your contacts before signing up to make sure the emails go to your inbox!

Did you know this book is also available in audio and paperback on all major retailers? Go to my website for links!

Trigger warnings in this title include prior off-page death of a sibling.

1

I CALL HER NANCY

Emerson

It's big. It's thick. It's delicious. And it's going in my mouth.

There's only one question.

"Will it fit?" I ask the sexy man across from me.

He smirks. Devilishly, of course. "Ah, the age-old question."

Time to find out. "Come to me, you juicy, delicious thing," I coo.

A dozen onlookers edge closer, staring at this big beauty and my lips. They aren't the only ones. A nearby camera records our scene as my co-host works the crowd. "Show of hands. Can she do it?"

"I've got this, Nolan. I've handled bigger," I say, all bravado and big mouth.

"I don't know. You're gonna have to prove it," Nolan taunts.

"Go ahead. Underestimate me." I relax my throat, part my lips, and then go in for the whole shebang.

I bite down, and wow. Just wow.

Involuntarily, I roll my eyes because this is tasty. With the camera on me, I indulge in another delicious bite.

"Yes," I moan around the double-decker veggie burger.

With a satisfied sigh, I set the flavor extravaganza on the plate. Picking up a napkin, I dab a bit of low-fat pesto from the corner of my lips. Low-calorie, that's our jam.

A boisterous redhead in the crowd offers a rocker salute. "Give it that *killer moan*," she calls out.

"It's your trademark, Veggie Girl," the wavy-haired brunette next to her chimes in.

Ah, my people.

They want what they want.

I wink at the women. "Mmm," I start, drawing out the moan for effect. The ladies cheer me on. Bless them. Just fucking bless them. Then I turn my attention to the glasses-wearing, hazel-eyed, dark-haired guy across from me at the table. "That was a good one," I say to my co-host in all things food, dining, and double meaning.

A smirk plays on his lips. "Should I get you a towel to clean up after that up-close-and-personal encounter with the Double O Burger?"

Harriet's Burger Hut doesn't hold back on the innuendo for its signature meals—one of the many reasons why this former hole-in-the-wall burger joint in the Mission District has become capital-T trendy.

"You're just jealous because these veggie burgers are always better than your *full beef injection* ones," I tease, and Nolan drops his head in his hand, laughing.

He turns to the camera perched on a tripod at the edge of the table. "Do you see what I have to put up with? The mouth on this one," he says, shaking his head.

"Oh, you love it," calls a woman with her black hair in a high ponytail.

"I do," he says in a stage whisper, then snaps his gaze back to me as we keep rolling. "Your mouth is the reason I get up in the morning."

I waggle a finger at him. "Proof that I'm not the only one with a naughty mind."

But YouTube shows cannot survive on innuendo alone. Setting my black-polished nail on the edge of the plate, I slide the veggie feast toward him. "Your turn. Try it."

Nolan picks up the burger slathered in mushrooms, pesto sauce, and gooey low-fat cheddar cheese, then takes a bite. He gives nothing away as he chews. So typical. He puts it down with a *whatever* shrug. "It's not bad."

I slap the table, playing it up. "Oh, come on. The Double O is toe-curling."

"It did seem like you were having a knee-weakening moment with the burger," he deadpans.

"Foodgasm!" the ponytail woman calls out.

With a big smile, I meet her eyes. "You know it!"

"Let me guess. *You'd do it again,*" Nolan says to me, imitating one of my catchphrases from the show.

I lean across the table and swat his shoulder. "You bet I would. Food is one of life's great pleasures, and some dishes demand encores."

"What are you gonna give it, then?"

I rub my palms, prolonging the suspense. Viewers love to predict our ratings. Later, we'll edit in a clock-ticking pause to give them the chance to place their drinking game bets as they watch.

Holding up a hand like I'm taking an oath, I issue my declaration: "On a scale of one to ten, I'm giving this bad boy a nine point four five."

Nolan barks out a laugh. "How long since you've rated anything under a nine, Em?"

"We pick well! We've been to some fab places. Why should I punish the food just because all these great dishes have raised the bar?"

"How can everything be close to a ten, though? You're such a Paula."

"And you're such a Simon. I don't grade food on a bell curve. Don't blame me for having excellent taste when scoping out spots for us to review." Ha. So there. I fold my arms across my chest, adopting a stern stare as my eyes stray to his empty plate. He ate the Full Monty Cheeseburger before I sampled the veg one. "And what are you giving your beef burger, Mister Mean Judge?"

A lazy shrug is his answer. And damn, he's good at those sexy shrugs. They reel in the viewers.

The man flings a careless glance at the carnivorous

carnage on his plate. "I can only give mine . . . a seven point two."

"You're such a hard judge," I tease.

"And you'd accept nothing less."

"That is true." I lift my veggie burger and take another bite, savoring the taste. Nolan watches the whole time, and as my tongue flicks against the corner of my lips, his hazel eyes darken a bit.

Maybe that's wishful thinking on my part.

Or dangerous thinking, really, the way those risqué thoughts come with a flutter in my chest.

Stupid flutter. Inconvenient thing.

I kick it aside. I won't let a flutter get in the way of my goals.

It's my turn to close out the episode, so I laser in on the camera. "And that's our review of Harriet's Burger Hut on this episode of *How to Eat a Banana*."

I stop recording with a flick of my finger, just like I stopped the flutters. Been doing both for years.

Next comes my favorite part of the job. Meeting fans always makes me feel like a big deal when I'm so not. But for a few minutes after we shoot, I can pretend.

I can pretend, too, that I've made all my dreams come true.

The fans who watched our live recording encircle us, equipped with cell phones and Sharpies. A fair-skinned redhead from the crowd bounces over to the table, along with a brunette with an olive complexion. "I just love you guys so much. Can we take a pic?"

With a twinkle in his eyes, Nolan flashes a panty-melting grin, aka his regular smile. "Only if you can be in it too," he says, all warm and inviting.

If flirting were a class, this man wouldn't just be the best student. He'd teach an expert course.

And every session would be packed.

The redhead blushes. "Yes, please," she says, then hands the phone to her friend.

I expect the woman to line up between Nolan and me, but she scoots next to him instead, her shoulder to his shoulder, nudging him closer to me. Her photo choreography leads to Nolan slinging an arm around me, which leads to my libido whispering dirty ideas about my friend and colleague.

So annoying, my overactive imagination, when she gets these wayward notions. I call her Nancy. A name makes backtalk much more satisfying.

When Nolan curls his hand around my shoulder, squeezing it, an irritating little burst of tingles kicks around in my chest.

Shut up, Nancy.

I smile for the camera phone.

When the picture is done, the redhead thrusts a purple Sharpie my way. "Can you both sign my shirt?"

I kind of can't believe we have any fans for this crazy endeavor, let alone ones who want me to mark their clothing in permanent ink. But the data doesn't lie, and more than one million YouTube subscribers tune in to our show. It still feels surreal.

The redhead spins around so we can sign her back.

I'm the good cop vegetarian, I write. And Nolan pens, *I'm the bad cop carnivore.*

After they take off, we chat with a few more fans and take pics with others as the waitstaff wipes down nearby tables, prepping to open again for the dinner crowd.

Finally, the rest of the fans filter out until only a perky blonde remains. "I'm Marie," she says, "and I just wanted to say you guys are so cute. When I heard you were shooting in the Mission, I left work early to meet you. I watch almost every episode with my sister."

A pang lashes my heart at the last word. "That must be so fun," I say, a little wistful.

"It is. We try all the local places you go to. And when you offer suggestions for an at-home equivalent, we rush out to the grocery store and grab those items to try too."

"Rock on, Marie." Nolan gives her that stomach-flipping smile. "And do you and your sister rate the food, as well?"

The woman beams. "Yes! We play along with what you guys do. We judge when you judge."

"So, are you the good cop or the bad cop?" I ask.

With a hint of a smile, her eyes drift to Nolan. "Bad cop. Like Nolan. And when I watch alone, I play along too," she says, directing those comments to my co-host as she bats her lashes at him, in all his bespectacled hotness.

I bet that's not all she's playing with when she watches him.

"You're my favorite YouTube star, Nolan," she gushes, clutching her chest, then she turns to me. "You're so lucky to be with him."

And here we go again.

With a kind laugh, Nolan shakes his head, pointing a thumb my way. "We're just friends."

It's the truth.

Except for that one night. But that was a few years ago, so who cares?

Not me.

And not Nancy.

The blonde seems delighted with this intel. "Oh, you're not?"

Nolan hauls me closer, hooking his arm around my shoulders. "Emerson is my BFF. She knows all my secrets," he whispers.

"Every last one," I say. That's how it goes with friends.

"That's very good to know," the cheery blonde says, and I bet in three, two, one, she'll ask him out.

I've seen this happen a thousand times before. I'm chill with it. So's Nancy.

Marie steps in front of me, her body language cutting me out of the scene. *Okay, Marie. Message received.*

"So, Nolan. Do you want to grab a coffee later?" she asks him with a twirl of her hair.

I inch away and out from under his arm, since, whatever. He's cute; ladies like him. I'm not territorial.

But even though I'm giving him space, I know his jam, and I mouth along as he answers her with a *gee-whiz* smile. "Wow, I appreciate the offer, Marie, but we've got to edit this episode. You wouldn't want me to miss posting it, would you, now?"

The man is good. He turns women down with so much honey in his voice it feels like a sugary compliment.

Some men are just talented like that.

"Of course I don't want you to miss posting," Marie says.

Ironic, since he's not the one who posts the videos. I am.

"Be sure to watch, though. We always try to include the audience shots. We love our viewers."

She giggles. "I love you, Nolan." Then, she peels away, beelining for the door.

"Love you too, Marie," I call out nicely since, sometimes, I'm secretly a dick.

"I'm sure she thinks you're great too," Nolan whispers near my ear.

"Oh yes, I'm so sure it was me she was loving on when she watched *alone*."

After we gather our bags and gear, we thank Harriet for letting us shoot in her fabulously divey joint.

The sturdy woman in the "Don't you dare kiss the chef" apron tuts. "I have you to thank. Business will be through the roof tomorrow. I already got triple the takeout orders in the last hour just from you posting you were shooting here." Then, she lowers her voice. "And that was some slick handling of those *are-you-together* questions. I love how you two pretend you're not a thing."

I scoff. "We're not. We're definitely not."

Nolan chuckles. "We're just friends, like we said."

Harriet winks. Twice. "Sure. Whatever you say."

I don't deny it again. People believe what they want to believe.

We head out onto the San Francisco street. "If only we could bottle their interest in us being together, we'd be rich," I joke.

"Bottle it and sell that shit. We'd definitely hit the next level," Nolan agrees, a note of longing in his voice.

I feel that longing deep in my chest. "We'll get there," I say, chin up.

The next level is a tough climb, though. Very few YouTubers make a decent living from web TV alone. But that's our goal—for the show to support us. To pay off our loans. Even with a million viewers, we aren't quite there yet.

We duck into a coffee shop a few blocks away, order some fuel, then set up a makeshift edit bay at a table. Once I have one macchiato in me and another close at hand, I edit with the kind of focus that would make a Nikon jealous. Meanwhile, Nolan is busy interacting with fans on social media.

An hour later, I spin my laptop around and show him the edit of today's episode, complete with the audience shots he promised Marie.

Nolan blows on his fingernails. "Damn, Em. Why are you so good at literally everything?"

"That's easy—YouTube," I answer.

"Is there anything you haven't taught yourself online?"

"Let's see." I count off on my fingers. "Learned how to edit videos, change a flat, juggle, and do a smoky eye. So, the answer is . . . no."

Peering intensely through those Clark Kent glasses, he checks out my eyes. Flames lick my cheeks from his hot stare. "You mean that kind of sexy, smudged eyeliner look?"

I catch my breath. "Yes. But I didn't do that today," I mumble.

"I think you look good with smoky eyelids and without," he says, his smile at full wattage.

I raise my deflector shield. I can't let Nolan's champion flirting get to me—or Nancy, for that matter. I'm all business as I say, "So, you're good with the episode? Can we post it?"

"Fire it up, baby," he says.

After I hit upload, I find him pointing at his computer screen like an animated character. "Whoa. Big news here. Like, super-big news."

"YouTube loves us and sent us an offer to be on the home page for a week?" I guess. "Oh, wait, I know! An organic food-maker signed on for a sah-weet sponsorship deal that'll change our lives?"

"Close. Very close. Try to control your excitement, but we did sell ten more *Foodgasm* T-shirts from our merch shop today," he says.

"Don't knock it. That helps. Every little bit does."

"Too true. By my calculations, if we sell seven thousand five hundred T-shirts, I might be able to pay off my student loans," he quips. But like most jokes, it contains a big kernel of truth.

"Stahp, stahp, that's crazy talk. No one has ever been able to do that in the history of ever," I say. I sure as shit haven't paid off mine.

Reflexively, I check our views. More than one thousand in the first minute. It'll tick higher—exponentially higher. Trouble is that the ad revenue on the views doesn't go that far.

Unless you break out big time.

And the chances of that are slim, so it's lucky I learned how to juggle because it's likely I'll be doing that with two jobs for a long time.

That evening, I walk into the pipsqueak apartment I used to share with my sister, my eyes drifting briefly to a five-by-seven picture on the coffee table in the living room—a framed photograph of Cadillac Ranch on Route 66. My chest tightens as I remember taking that picture two years ago, and I look away, focusing on clicking the door closed behind me.

My couch pillows call out to me, but I resist their siren song. Instead, I drop my messenger bag onto a metal chair at my kitchen table and perform my presto-chango routine.

Voila.

Fifteen minutes later, I'm freshened up and decked out all in black—the makeup artist's unofficial dress code. After a quick jaunt across the city to a luxury hotel in Union Square, I spend the next hour in the penthouse suite painting the faces of a quartet of eighteen-year-old girls from the city's fanciest private school.

"Oh my God, we look so good for prom. You're straight fire with a makeup brush," a gal named Bexley coos at me.

"It's easy when I have such a good canvas," I say. I mean, hello, perfect dewy teenage skin.

Makeup is fun, but I figured I'd be done with these freelance gigs by age thirty. That by now, the show would cover all my bills and then some. Dreams are hard to catch, though, no matter how tenaciously you chase them.

I swipe some glittery blush on Tilly, and she declares I "slayed it." I know what she means, though I don't try to adopt their lingo, since . . . not cool.

Once I'm done, I thank the girls then pack up, checking the time as the elevator sweeps me to the lobby.

If I scurry two blocks over to California Street, I can catch the bus back to my place before the new murder mystery premiers on Hulu at nine. I'll text Katie and Jo. See if they want to do a watch party. We can place bets on twists. Yup, some friends, a glass of wine, a pair of soft PJ pants, and a chance to escape with my girls into a twisty, zany story are just what the doctor ordered.

But as I turn the corner, the blue bus trundles away.

Ugh.

My shoulders sag, and I trudge all the way to the covered stop, the makeup bag digging into my hip. As I wait for the next bus, I idle away the minutes on my phone, rewatching today's episode—particularly the moments after I bit into the veggie burger.

I did not imagine it—when Nolan watched me lick my lips, his dreamy eyes did darken.

A tingle swoops down my chest, but I squash it down.

Cool it, Nancy. You're not in charge.

2

MAKE YOURSELF DECENT, JAYBIRD

Nolan

It's weird sometimes, the pervasive idea that you can do anything. Be anything.

Can you, though? Most careers require a little thing called talent to get started.

Check. We've got that.

Then, there's potential. Sure, we're swimming in it, the way our viewer and subscriber numbers keep beautifully rising.

But leaving aside skill and opportunity, the hard reality is that you *can* do anything, but you can't *keep* doing it if your "anything" isn't making enough money.

Emerson and I are horseshoe close. The dice roll we made on a fun, flirty food-judging show where we also offer food-shopping tips is nipping at the heels of success.

But the show needs to take off really fucking soon because I'm running out of time to pay the piper.

I walk home from the coffee shop that evening, my legs eat up the sidewalk, and my mind flashes frenetically forward three months to *that* date—the looming day when an unexpected debt comes due.

Surprise! The joke was on me, and now the thought of my dirty little secret IOU is making me walk faster and driving me to work harder on the show all the time.

If I don't, I'll have to fight the millions of foodie wannabes for a job as a line cook. Maybe a sous chef if I'm lucky.

I shudder. Restaurant life is not for me. Been there, done that, have the scars from it. Not to mention it's fuck-all hard to afford your own place on the pay—last time I worked that gig, I had three roommates in an eight-hundred-square-foot apartment with bad plumbing.

As the chichi Pacific Heights neighborhood comes into view, I cycle through possible next steps to skyrocket *How to Eat a Banana* into the stratosphere.

Enter a killer contest?

Nab a new sponsorship?

Pair up with an influencer?

I plan to spend the rest of the evening brainstorming the above like I do most nights. That's what I'm thinking about as I bound up the steps to a sleek, modern townhome on Jackson Street.

Swinging open the door to my brother's swank pad, I call out, "Better make yourself decent, Jaybird. Don't want to have to buy any bleach to wash out my eyes."

No answer—the house is still. Jason's probably out for a run, so I toss the keys on the foyer table a decorator picked out for him along with the big-screen TV, the U-shaped couch, and the wet dream of a kitchen. The appliances in this place get me going.

"This is your last warning. You are not alone. You are now in the presence of your older, hotter, smarter brother."

More silence, so I've got the place to myself. But warnings are good, if not essential. The other week, I walked in right as a hookup of his was walking out.

In the kitchen, I settle in with my tablet at the counter, ignoring the temptation of the stove as I check out some other online channels for ad ideas. When I have a list of potential sponsorships, I fire it off to my friend and agent.

Hayes is on it; the dude replies right away with, *Speak of the devil. I had some good calls today about your show.*

Were you going to keep that intel to yourself? He wouldn't recognize me if I didn't give him a hard time.

Another quick reply: *No, smartass. I didn't tell you because I've been racing to catch my flight to LA to meet peeps on your behalf. I just boarded and this is the first chance I've had. But thanks for the vote of confidence. And just so you know, I met with a cattle farmer today, and he wants to peddle manure on your show. I said yes for ya. Cool?*

I crack my knuckles and type, *That's why you get the . . . little bucks.*

I get a middle-finger emoji, but that's what I deserve

for hiring my buddy as an agent for Em and me, even if the guy is a wunderkind.

Hayes sends one more note: *Anyway, I had some good calls. Just talking you up with streaming services and producers. Irons, baby. I've got 'em in the fire.*

I pump a fist then write back: *Very well. I'll keep you for now.*

Next, I toggle over to YouTube and log into our dashboard. And *whoa.*

Check this out.

There's a message to all top creators titled *Everything's Better in Pairs! Collab Up!* I scan the message to get the gist. The goal is to link similar shows that garner lots of views. You choose a partner, and it's easy as pie—you recommend each other's work for a week or so. If YouTube likes what you do, it goes on the home page.

Cha-ching.

This smells like a jackpot, the type of opportunity that could push us over the cusp where we've sat for so long. I've been living on the motherfucking cusp for so long I've got squatter's rights.

The brink of success is sharp and uncomfortable, but it keeps me hungry. Then again, so does my belly. It's been eight hours since burger time, so I set down the tablet and amble over to my brother's fancy-ass Sub-Zero fridge.

I stroke the door and sigh because the brushed steel feels so good. "You're a babe," I tell the sexy silver beast before yanking open the door.

I peruse the offerings laid out neatly and orderly. Chicken breast. Tofu. Kale. Quinoa. Broccoli.

Can someone say *my brother's a health nut?*

But then again, so am I.

Oh. Look at that. "Shishito peppers. My little bro loves me," I say, and right as I grab the bowl of fresh green goodies, the front door whooshes open.

"That's debatable," a voice calls out.

As Jason saunters in, I shake my head. "There is no debate. These peppers are proof." I point at the shelf. "You love me more than any other brother."

"Not much competition when you're the only person entered. You basically walk away with first place."

I brandish the veggie as evidence. "You got my fave snack ever. I call that brotherly love. Obviously, you want to keep me around." I set the bowl on the sleek, black counter as if daring him to argue, but mostly I want to hear him say he enjoys me hanging around at his place.

I feel like a freeloader because I am. Before I returned to San Francisco a couple of months ago, I spent some time in New York, crashing at my friend TJ's place. Couch surfing is a special skill, but not one I've honed by choice.

With a dismissive wave, Jason doesn't even nibble on the bait. "Nah, those peppers are accidental. The food delivery company must have sent them over by mistake."

Narrowing my eyes, I wag a finger at my taller, broader, younger bro. "You worship the ground I walk on, and this is your offering," I counter.

In a blur worthy of a cheetah going for a Serengeti

kill, Jason steps forward, whips off my glasses, then wraps his hands around my head. Fucker cages me into an MMA move in less than three seconds. "Say it. *I know the peppers were just coincidental, Jaybird,*" he says, and holy fuck. He's stronger than I thought. I seem to have forgotten my five years on him mean jack shit to his gridiron-hardened muscles.

But I am stubborn-er.

"They were on purpose. A gift to me," I mutter.

He breaks out the big guns, rubbing his knuckles against my skull, and that's not fair. "No noogies," I protest.

"Noogies till you admit the truth."

I won't, I won't, I won't. I try to wriggle out of his chokehold, but hey, I guess the San Francisco Hawks knew what they were doing when they locked him up. His hands are vises.

No choice but to throw in the towel. "The peppers were accidental. You didn't get them for me," I grumble.

Jason relents, letting go, then patting my shoulders and smoothing my vintage Roxy Music shirt. "I see we agree at last," he says, then grabs my glasses and hands them to me.

I slide them back on with a huff. "Then we can agree that I'll cook up these accidental peppers all by my lonesome then."

He growls for a good long while. "Fine, I got you those peppers since you love them. Also, you're really fucking good at making them. So, can you, you know, get cooking?" He eyes the skillet on the stove, pasting on a *please cook for me* grin, and I don't feel like a schlub anymore.

"Course I will," I say, then clap his back. "Want some chicken too? I found a new kale and chicken recipe that will make you salivate."

He nods. "Pretty please."

Personal chef I am and happy to do it. He's let me crash here for almost a month, no questions asked. Though, the brother code dictates I can't let on that I like being his cook. *Must give him shit.* "Knew you loved me bunches," I say, then while he takes off to shower, I whip up dinner, sautéing the chicken and the kale.

A little later, with wet hair from the shower this time, he pads back into the kitchen as the veggies sizzle. "What have you been up to today?" he asks as he yanks open the fridge and grabs a bubbly water.

"I found a cool new contest to enter."

"Is it for the hottest YouTube stars?"

"Ha." I roll my eyes because sure, I made that list, and it did give us a boost for a bit. It also gave my friends and family endless fodder to tease me. Fair game, I suppose. "I only wish those paid well. If they did, I'd clean up."

He cracks open the can and takes a sip. "So, what's the contest?"

"You pair up with other top creators," I say and give him the details. "So now, I'm just trying to decide who to reach out to. There's The Burger Boys, Pizza Paulie, Drive-Thru Babe . . . oh, and the Wine Dude. He's hilarious with his wine and food pairings for idiots."

Jason's blue eyes spark, and he sets down his drink

on the counter and snaps his fingers. "I have the perfect duo for you."

"You do? Who?" I ask, a little surprised since I don't think he spends his free time chilling with online videos unless they're of the game film variety or feature new yoga poses for football flexibility.

"I met these adorable grandmas at a signing the other week. They are so freaking cute. You're going to love them. *Dot and Bette's Home-Cooked Meals*."

"Oh yeah! I've heard of them. They started a few months ago and shot all the way up, but I haven't checked them out yet since their style is so different." I toss him a side-eye glare as I turn down the heat, then slide the peppers into a bowl. "But what the hell? I can't believe you watched another food show."

"Another? You assume I watch yours," he deadpans.

I heave a sigh. "Why do I root for you?"

"Because I'm awesome, and I'm also your favorite brother," he points out.

"Participation trophy for you too, Jaybird," I say, but truth be told, this guy has done more for me than any brother should. Hell, I could say the same for my dad. The men in my family are all the way awesome, and I'd just like to live up to one-tenth of who they are. Maybe I will if I can get the hell off the damn cusp.

I sprinkle some salt and pepper on the green yummies, then put the bowl on the counter. "Let's check out some Dot and Bette while we eat," I say, plating his dinner next, then cueing up the ladies on the tablet and crunching into a fantastic pepper.

The screen fills with the welcoming faces of two

sixty-something women. One is Black, one is white, and both wear gingham dresses.

"Well, hello there, y'all. I'm Dot. And I don't believe in the gospel of butter, olive oil, or too much fat. I worship at the altar of healthy-ish meals," the white woman says in a big Texas accent.

The Black woman goes next, her voice pure Georgia charm. "And I'm Bette, and you can bet your bottom dollar we'll teach you every dang thing we know about how to substitute applesauce in chocolate chip cookies without a single soul but your priest knowing."

Holy shit.

They are sassy and on the same wavelength when it comes to healthy eating. They're like your favorite feisty grandmas.

"They're good," I say after a few videos and a few more of the life-sustaining peppers.

"They also love *me*," Jason says, setting down his fork, then pointing to their recent episode.

I groan, but it's a proud groan when I click on that one.

And what do you know? Dot and Bette are both sporting my brother's Hawks jersey—signed by the dude who threw footballs to *me* in the backyard. I was his favorite target growing up, and that still makes me proud.

"So, we are super excited because we met Jason McKay last week, and yes, hold your horses, friends, he signed my jersey," Dot says and turns around to show off a number fourteen.

"And to think I signed a T-shirt in a burger shop

today," I mutter. But these ladies? A few short months on the site, and they've already shot past us in viewership. They're YouTube darlings, getting love from the site and from sponsors. They'd be ideal partners.

Jason nudges me with his elbow. "Tell them you're my bro. I bet they'd love to partner with you," he says, then finishes his dinner.

This kid, he's smart. I send Dot and Bette an email asking if they want to collaborate.

In the morning, there's a reply for me, and I can't decide if I'm thrilled or terrified to open it.

3

MISTER HUSTLE

Nolan

Emerson gives good "excited" face.

I've seen many versions of it since I met her twelve years ago at college.

There was the time in junior year when she scored nosebleed tickets to *Les Mis* on Broadway and belted out her own lyrics to "One Day More" in our dorm hall:

ToMORrow I'LL be in Times Squaaaaare . . .

And WITH this SHOW a fangirl has starteeeeeehhhd.

Then, a couple of years ago, when the first episode of *How to Eat a Banana* reached a thousand views in two hours, she moonwalked on Fillmore Street. Though, full disclosure, I dared her to, since the day before, she'd bragged about learning how to moonwalk from a series of Michael Jackson dance-move tutorials.

Earlier this year, when she was having a rough day, I

surprised her by whipping up her favorite sandwich in the whole world—avocado, Beecher's Cheese, tomatoes, and my very own signature sauce on an everything baguette from the Sunshine Bakery. With a smile of gratitude, she crunched into it, moaned around it, and then set it down to throw her arms around me. "This sandwich makes me so happy," she'd said.

Maybe I glowed a little from the compliment.

But those moments pale next to the way her face splits into a city-wide smile as she grabs my phone and reads the email, wonder in her irises.

We're standing in the financial district outside the TV station where she's just finished doing makeup for the morning show anchor. Wind whips by, a typical San Francisco chill in the spring air.

Once she finishes reading, she says, "Allow me," then adopts a Texas down-home accent and reads it again, this time aloud.

Dear Nolan,

What an absolute delight to hear from you. Wouldn't you know, but we're big fans of your show. We just started watching it last night, and we did that binge-y thing! Woohoo! And we sure like what we see. You and your little lady are so stinking cute.

We would love to partner with you. What a treat to meet someone who doesn't cook Paula Deen style! You've got to keep that ticker going for the more fun activities in life! As I say, food is fuel for love.

If you know what I mean.

Winky face!

So, here's the story. Our business manager, Evelyn, is here with us in Vegas. And we're throwing a little ol' party tomorrow since we just crossed some threshold or another on the YouTube. What a fun site! But . . . Confession time: We don't even know how to get on the YouTube.

Evelyn does all the uploads and the videos and the thingies behind the scenes. We just smile for the camera and stir up the blessings in the kitchen.

In any case, we like to do everything face-to-face. We don't suppose you'd want to come to our party tomorrow night? I think you're in California, so maybe just hop in a convertible and road trip on across the state border! Come join us, and we could even shoot a quick video too, for both our channels, assuming all goes well!

It's kind of last-minute, but hey, sometimes the best things in life are spontaneous. Like my grilled zucchini nachos! I'll be serving them tomorrow night!

All my best,

Dot, Bette's best friend

Emerson thrusts the phone back at me, and I drop it into my pocket, rocking on my toes and asking, "So, what do you think?"

"What do I think?" She'd be rubbish at poker; she can't bluff for beans.

"Yes, what did you think?" I repeat. She looks as if she's about to take off for Jupiter, but I want to hear it from the woman herself. This chance means as much to her as it does to me. And if I can make success happen for both of us, well, that would go a long way toward making up for dumb decisions in my past.

Her brown hair blows in the breeze, and she flicks it back and advances slowly toward me, a sly grin playing on her lips. Her eyes are sparklers, twin fireworks on the Fourth of July. My best friend looks happier than she did when I made her that sandwich, so it might be time for me to revise my list of Top Excited Emerson Face Moments.

"I think . . . *Vegas, baby, Vegas*. I think . . . let's make a deal with these two ladies. They're huge, and their show is all that. I think this is one of the best things ever and you"—she pokes my chest—"are officially amazing."

I feel fucking amazing too, like we're closing in on our dreams coming true.

She lifts her hands for a double high-five. We smack palms, and . . . wait.

I didn't expect her to do *that*.

She's not letting go. My gaze sails down to our joined hands, her fingers curled through mine, clasping tight to me outside the TV studio building. "Holy shit, Nolan," she whispers, as if to voice it at full volume would be too risky. As if we need to guard our hopes in secret a little longer or life might vanquish them again.

"Holy shit, indeed," I whisper back, excitement thrumming through me.

If we pull this off. If it lands us on the home page.

If, if, if.

This could be our next step. The thing that gets us

out of debt. The thing that makes this a full-time gig for us.

I squeeze her fingers too, and like this, with our faces inches apart, I'm thinking we're going to kiss again.

My pulse surges, and for a couple of dangerous seconds, I imagine us kissing again here on a street corner in the city, on a chilly morning, in this bubble of possibility.

A we-might-just-pull-this-off kiss.

But a few seconds after that risqué thought stirs things up south of the border, she lets go. "I need to make a to-do list."

Saved by her idiosyncrasies. "Yes, yes you do," I say.

My voice is a little rough from that momentary meander. I shake it off and adjust my glasses, even though they don't need adjusting.

Emerson, though, is all business. Guess I'm the only one who tripped back in time to that past kiss.

"We need to be in Vegas tomorrow night." She points to the street, shorthand for "time to walk and talk." We get moving as she lays out our plan of attack. "Here's what we need to do. Book our travel, pack an overnight bag, get a hotel."

"A cheap one," I add.

"Obviously."

"We'll grab our gear and plan a fantastic concept for a quickie episode to run on our channels. Wait, wait! I already have one." She spins to walk backward, that gigantic makeup bag swinging like a blunt weapon by her side. "We need something super Vegas-y. Ooh, how about we swing by Tacos El Gordo? The double corn tortillas there are supposed to be a religious experience."

"I do believe," I say like I've gone Pentecostal.

A victorious yes comes from her lips as she wheels around again. "Heavenly tacos will pave the way to their hearts."

This episode idea is good, but it can be better. After all, can man and woman live on tacos alone? "Better yet. How about we bring Dot and Bette a sampler of our Vegas faves? To taste test on camera with them if they're game. We can get Brussels sprouts from Momofuku, tacos from Tacos El Gordo, and egg sandwiches from—"

We shout in unison, "The Egg Slut."

Emerson stops at the curb. "Shut up, just shut up," she says, practically vibrating with excitement.

I arch a brow. "You really want me to shut up?"

"Shut up and let me praise you, Mister Hustle. That's what I'm going to call you. And you pulled this off while I was sleeping."

With a cocky grin, I rub my fingernails against my shirt. "Brains and beauty, baby. This guy has it all."

With a bump of her shoulder to mine, she says, "I know, trust me. I know you've got it all."

There's a note of wistfulness in her voice, but I'm not sure what to make of it, especially when we resume our pace and her makeup bag slips down her shoulder, inching along her arm.

"Let me help you," I say, then tug at the strap.

She shakes her head. "You don't have to."

I scoff. "Don't have to what? Be nice and carry your fifty-million-pound bag?"

She tilts her head, flapping a hand at me. "Be . . . you know . . . all helpful with me."

But why wouldn't I be? "You don't want me to be helpful?"

"Like, manly helpful. You know what I mean," she says, dipping her face.

"I'm not sure I do. You mean like a boyfriend?"

She swallows visibly. "Yes. Friends don't have to carry their friends' makeup bags."

"The lack of sense in that life law is astonishing," I say. "Because that's exactly what friends do, you stubborn creature. And yes, I know you can do it yourself. I pretty much assume you can do everything yourself." I wiggle my fingers. "But I want to carry it. So gimme the bag, Miss DIY."

With a faux grumble, she hoists it off her shoulder and hands it to me. "Fine, Mister Hustle. Be that way."

I slide it on my shoulder, smiling in a most satisfied fashion. "I will."

"Also, thank you," she says softly.

"You're welcome, and you'll really thank me when I throw out ten thousand lipstick tubes from here tonight. You need to be an ox to carry this."

She rolls her shoulders back and forth like she's grateful the weight is gone. "Yes, you do, and I would never throw out a lipstick. You never know when it might be the right color. So, thank you for being friendly and manly and oxen-like." She rubs her palms together, ready to get cracking. "So, how are we going to do this? Airline?"

I grimace. "I already checked. It's around six hundred dollars a ticket since it's last minute."

"Ouch. Road trip then? I do love a good road trip."

"I know you do. But . . ." I tap my chin. "There's only one little problem."

She deals me a stern stare. "Don't tell me you have something against Wanda?"

"No. Not at all," I say in exaggerated denial. "I don't have anything against the world's smallest car. I love having my knees scrunched up by my eyes." I do my best impression of the kind of sardine-like maneuver I'd have to execute to fold myself into the passenger seat of her wheels.

"It's a little car, I'll admit. But Wanda is a relentless beast," she says, then goes quieter. "And she was Callie's."

"And I get that Wanda's special because it was your road-trip car," I say, squeezing her shoulder as we cross the street.

Emerson shudders out a breath, then rolls her shoulders. "And Wanda did her service," she says, fondness in her tone now. "Grand Canyon, Chain of Rocks Bridge, Cadillac Ranch." She emits a low whistle. "I mean, that car deserves a medal. Who knew it could hit all the classic Route 66 tour stops?"

I shrug an *I told you so*. "Not to pat myself on the back, but I did tell you to go for it."

She laughs, bumping our shoulders together. "You did, and I'm glad we made that trip. Anyway, Wanda is an option, but maybe not for a Daddy Long Legs like you. And I'd ask if we could borrow Jason's Tesla roadster, but I once googled the price of those, and there's no way I'd let you borrow your brother's wheels."

"Good, because I'd never ask. He already does enough by letting me crash at his sweet pad," I say, a little embarrassed, even though Emerson knows the score. "Not to mention that he paid for culinary school."

"And you know he was happy to do that," she says.

But I wish I could do something for him. Yes, he was a first-round draft pick and got a huge bonus, and when he knew I wanted to go to cooking school, he didn't just offer to pay. He pretty much begged me to let him. And here I am, a few years later, without a restaurant or a chef's hat to show for his generosity.

"I'm sure he was real happy that I went and decided a few years later that I didn't like being a chef," I say drily.

"I think he's happy if you're happy, but I hear you, and I think we should just rent a car," she says, clicking around on her phone, then she sighs heavily. Her brow knits. "Did you know it's nine hours to drive? We'll have to leave tonight just to be safe, and we'll need two nights at a hotel then. Are you sure there aren't any cheap flights?" she asks as a sign for Doctor Insomnia's Tea and Coffee Emporium beckons us at the end of the block.

"I'm sure I'll think better with an espresso with two sugars," I offer.

We duck into the shop, order, then hunt for a last-minute deal.

"Ooh!" Emerson thrusts her hand in the air. "Found one."

"What's the damage?"

"Sixty-nine dollars round trip."

I waggle my eyebrows. "My inner twelve-year-old can't resist commenting."

"Find the will, Nolan."

"C'mon! I can't. *You said sixty-nine*. It's a sign. I have to mention the sixty-nine."

She rolls her eyes. "Are we doing this?"

"Sixty-nining?" I ask innocently. Because what choice do I have?

But the way her face flashes pink like she's having heatstroke makes me wonder all sorts of things. Like, did I just embarrass the woman who jokes about her big mouth and how much she can take? Like, is she thinking about sex too?

But I promised myself one night in Vegas a few years ago that I'd do my damnedest to stop thinking about Emerson naked.

I haven't entirely kept that promise, though I try. I try as hard as I can.

Her chestnut hair falls in a curtain around her face as she taps away on the screen. "Okay. There are two seats left on Bacon Grease Airlines."

"Bacon Grease?" I ask with an eyebrow arch, zooming in on the to-do list, not my to-entertain-dirty-thoughts-of list.

"I figure that's what they serve on this airline. Bacon grease and cigarette butts for breakfast."

"Sounds upscale to serve anything at all these days," I quip as she swipes the screen.

"At this price, we'll have to stand the whole flight. You don't mind, do you?"

"It's gonna be like one of those old-school amusement park rides where you press your back against a wall panel."

"The Gravitron. It's Gravitron Airlines, and they serve you bacon grease," she says.

"Wow. I can't wait," I deadpan.

"Me neither," she says.

But the thing is, I'm not lying. I can't freaking wait. Call me crazy, call me Mister Hustle, call me A Hopeful Guy, but this chance with Dot and Bette feels like it could lead to me saying sayonara to the cusp in the nick of time.

And doing it all with my best-friend-turned-business-partner?

That's no problem whatsoever.

* * *

The next day, we board our flight, like a couple of eager, first-time travelers.

"Vegas, baby, Vegas," I say, channeling Vince Vaughn as we grab our seats. It's hammy even for me, but I want to make Vegas feel like just any party destination, not the place where Emerson and I shared that kiss.

Okay, fine. Maybe I just want to pretend I don't still wish for one more.

4

THE PUNCHLINE PARROTS

Emerson

We hurtle toward the sky in the world's noisiest plane, sandwiched in our seats like rolled-up T-shirts in a how-to-pack-a-suitcase video. My right thigh is wedged come-up-and-see-me-sometime style against Nolan's. My left thigh is smushed against the window seat man, who apparently bathed in Drakkar Noir this morning.

But it's a short flight. We'll be there in a jiffy, the cheery flight attendant has informed us.

Too bad I'm as jittery as if I've been mainlining coffee.

Only, I didn't have any.

And I'm not usually a nervous flier.

So, what's the deal?

Maybe it's the tin-can feel of this plane. I consider reading a book to blot out this new noise in my head. Or I could watch that how to make your own jam series

I downloaded last week or rewatch all the Dot and Bette videos in their library. I've seen a bunch of their episodes, and I watched all of them last night, but I'm a prepper and it wouldn't hurt to have them fresh in my mind.

Trouble is, any of those options would require contorting my body like a cartoon character to grab my phone from my backpack. There's maybe six inches of legroom, so that seems risky. Best just to chat with my traveling companion, even though he's enrapt with a fierce game of solitaire.

"Question," I say as he swipes a card on a stack. "What are the chances the plane will tilt if I grab my phone? How precariously do you think this contraption is balanced?"

Nolan slides a six of clubs onto the seven of diamonds, not looking up from the screen. "Chances are high. Best to stay still the entire flight."

"Cool, cool. It's like an MRI tube, then," I say.

"That's dark." He chuckles as he adds a five to the stack, then the four.

"We're on the world's cheapest airline for humans. We're well past dark. Did you read the fine print on the tickets?"

"Who reads the fine print?" He snags the three now, then the two.

I stick my thumb against my chest; I can just move it that far. "Me."

"Of course you do."

"What does that mean?"

Finally, something that warrants a look—he lifts his eyes from the screen, his expression amused. "Em, you are such a fine-print person."

"Life is all about the fine print," I say.

"Life is about the why not," he counters, but the twitch in his lips says he might be egging me on.

The twitch also tells me he enjoys it.

"Oh, please," I say, enjoying it too. "If all you do is say why not, then you're gonna get screwed."

"You might get screwed anyway."

"And I didn't want to get screwed over on the flight, so I checked the fine print for hidden fees. It said the 'cheapest airline for humans.'"

"Ah, that tracks now," he says, with a tip of his forehead to the back of the plane before turning to his phone once more.

This puddle jumper is egalitarian when it comes to passengers. A couple of dogs are seat-belted in a few rows back, and in front of them, some cats travel in carriers. When I was boarding, I also spotted some metal crates in the back row.

I hope they don't contain snakes. Indiana Jones and I have a lot in common, and neither of us likes slithery animals.

A dog barks, deep and booming.

"Sounds like a Great Dane. I hope he got two seats," I say, tapping my fingers against the denim on my thighs.

That gets Nolan's attention—the tapping. He looks away from his game and at me. "Are you nervous?"

I scoff. "No. C'mon. We've flown before. I usually just nap."

"And you're not sleeping now. So, I'll ask again. Are you nervous?"

A cat behind us meows. Sounds like she's saying *meow-yes.*

Stop reading my mind, cat.

It's just *this* flight that's rattling me. The incessant hum of the tube hurtling through the clouds. "Nah, I'm fine," I say, even as a voice in my head whispers *liar*.

Nolan squeezes my thigh, an affectionate gesture that elicits . . . goose bumps.

Just what I didn't need.

A dose of shivery tingles that make me think of . . .

Nope. Won't go there.

"We'll land soon," Nolan reassures me. Then he offers me his phone. "Want to play?"

"No, I'll just watch you play solitaire. Since that's not creepy at all," I say drily.

Another squeeze of my thigh. Another blast of sparklers along my skin. "Be a creeper, Em. Do it," he urges.

I sigh, aggrieved, and watch as he goes back to moving cards like a solitaire shark.

A swipe here. A play there. I stare mindlessly, settling for any distraction. I am wound up more than usual, more than this plane trip warrants.

Maybe it's because traveling with another person is strangely intimate. You learn things—like whether someone handles bumps in the road like a rickety old car or a smooth pair of wheels.

But don't I already know Nolan's style? We've flown together for the show a few times. A year ago, a food delivery app sponsored us for a month and sent us to Miami to review a ton of beach food trucks there.

In Florida, I discovered I'm the we-have-to-get-here-at-this-time person, while Nolan is the no-worries-it's-all-good one. All month, I made sure we didn't miss a single stop for our sponsor. Then on the last day on that trip, when traffic backed up on the Rickenbacker causeway and I was about to burst with worry over missing an appointment, Nolan found the perfect Jimmy Buffett tune to settle my nerves.

But he never played solitaire on that trip.

Is that why I'm jittery today? Because I didn't know this about him till now? I know so many things, but not everything, of course. There are always new quirks to discover about a person.

Suddenly, this detail feels vital. "Have you always played solitaire?" I blurt out.

He finishes the game with a final swipe, giving a small fist pump as the screen fills with *You beat the clock!*

"Yes. I play it for luck," he says.

"Have you always?"

"Used to play it when we traveled on family trips, like when we went to Jason's championships and stuff. I joked that he won because I played solitaire before his games like a lucky ritual."

That's a sweet image, and it tugs at my heart, their closeness. "Did he believe you?"

Nolan shrugs with a smile. "When he was younger, he did."

"He idolized you," I say, smiling now too.

"Maybe. Anyway, I stopped playing a while ago. Just lost interest, I guess. But this morning, I remembered it once felt lucky to me, so I broke it out again."

And I bet I know why. "You figured we could use some luck?"

His eyes lock with mine, those hazels flickering with unsaid words—*isn't it obvious we do?* "Yeah," he says aloud. "Since you've become even more superstitious lately, maybe together we can double our luck."

I jerk my chin back. "You think I've gotten *more* superstitious?"

He clears his throat. "In the last few months, I've seen you pick up pennies on the street for good luck, stop to take pictures of rainbows—and now you avoid ladders too."

"That's just good sense. Ladders are dangerous." I fiddle absently with the ladybug charm on my necklace.

His eyes drift to my throat, sweeping over the brushed metal on my skin, almost as if he were touching it. A flash of heat inconveniently spreads over my skin. "That too. Your ladybug. They're a sign of luck. Maybe we'll get lucky on this trip."

That's not why I wear the necklace, but I don't dispel him of that notion. A plane isn't the best place to talk about luck.

Or the first time we were in this city together.

That time a few years ago felt like the luckiest night ever. We hadn't yet experienced the desperation that wanting something just out of reach can bring you.

Now, I feel desperate in too many ways.

And yeah, I've got my answer.

That's why I'm a human espresso cup today. I want too many things.

"I hope we get lucky too," I say, "with this chance we're taking."

A scratching sound blares through the speakers. There's a pause, and I cock my head, waiting for more.

"Hello, ladies, gentlemen, boys and girls, and all creatures great and small. We've reached our cruising altitude, so let's give a big Super Saver Airlines shout-out to Lance McGruber, my co-pilot. Today marks his first flight ever."

Screw not being a nervous flier. I am entirely comprised of worry. I turn to Nolan. "What the . . .?"

His irises register curiosity right as the speaker crackles again.

"JK! JK!" says the voice over the speaker. "Lance can do this route with his eyes closed," the man warbles. "In fact, he's blindfolded right now."

Nolan rolls his eyes. "It's open mic night up front."

"Evidently," I say, the tension easing.

Maybe this is what I need. A good, old-fashioned distraction so my thoughts don't stray to the past.

The present is all that matters.

"He's been flying the Super Saver skies for twenty years. So, sit back, relax, and enjoy our special Super Saver snack service," says the pilot.

Wait a sexy second. "No one told me there would be snacks," I say to Nolan, latching onto this new intel.

"I didn't know they were offering your favorite meal of the day," he says.

Seriously. Snacks are life. I am shook. "Imagine if they have seaweed snacks, veggie chips, hummus and dip." I sigh happily.

He laughs. "You're adorable when you fantasize."

This convo is much better than talk of luck, chances, and desperate hope.

In the aisle, a flight attendant carries a beverage tray slung around her neck like a ballpark vendor peddling beer.

I nod her way and whisper to Nolan, "I'm not only thinking of snacks. I'm also thinking of what we can do with them."

He cackles with delight. "You. Me. Same wavelength." He tries to point from his chest to mine but can hardly maneuver his arm. "Do we have room to shoot an episode?"

"We'll make room. It'll be an up-close-and-personal rating of the snacks." This is brilliant. Not only will the rest of the flight pass quickly, but I can edit the episode while he drives us around the city. Then I won't have to think about the fact that we'll be sleeping down the hall from each other tonight.

The flight attendant stops at our row, batting her glittery blue eyelids at us, her twin pigtails bouncing. "Would you like a Super Saver Cola? A Super Saver Diet Cola? Or a fresh bottle of delicious water?"

With a straight face, Nolan views the offerings in her case. The cans are silver with black writing—in Comic Sans. They look so . . . fake. "So many choices."

The attendant smiles wanly.

Nolan's shrug translates to *why not take a free drink*. "I'll have a Diet Cola, please."

"Water for me," I add.

"Great. That'll be twenty dollars."

Whoa. Those are hotel minibar prices. Must have heard her wrong. "Excuse me," I say warily. "Did you say twenty dollars? Are you sure?"

She nods decisively. "Yes, ten dollars a drink. If you want ice, it's five dollars extra."

Hold all the horses.

"You charge for the ice," Nolan says staccato, each word laden with the full weight of shock.

"Yes, we do. Because ice is cool," she says blandly, like that's her go-to line every single time because she probably says it to every single passenger.

I guess this is how Super Saver Airlines can afford to have such cheap tickets.

"Thanks, but I'll pass," I say.

She lifts her case higher to show us some snack bags. Each is plain white with bold writing. "Want some pretzels?"

"What's the damage on those bad boys?" Nolan asks.

"Fifteen a bag," she says.

He whistles. "A veritable bargain."

Damn. This snack racket would pay off my loans in no time. But there goes the airplane food review plan. I won't spend that much for a shtick, and neither will Nolan. I didn't know about my best friend's solitaire good luck habit, but I'd bet all my makeup brushes he'll turn down the ridiculously priced snacks.

"No, thanks," Nolan says.

Yup. I was right.

"Let me know if you change your minds," the flight attendant says, then peers across me to the guy in the window seat.

The Drakkar Noir guy comes alive, his salacious eyes sailing up to the attendant. "I'll take your number, sweetheart," he says in a voice thicker than a shag carpet.

"That's not for sale. But the pretzels are good," she says wearily, like she's heard it a million times from guys doused in too much cologne.

Drakkar Noir doesn't hesitate. He fishes a couple bills from his wallet and thrusts them to her. "And a cola too."

"Great," she says, then hands him the goodies and continues down the aisle.

I stare wistfully at his drink for a second, then turn back to Nolan and rasp like I'm crawling across the sand in the desert, "So . . . thirsty . . ."

"Try to hold on, soldier. We'll stop at a 7-Eleven after we land. We can review the Slurpees and pretzels there."

"Not. Sure. If. I. Can. Make. It." I drop my head onto his shoulder.

He pats my head.

That's sort of nice and comforting.

What if he stroked my hair, though? Would nice and comforting level up to yummy and enticing?

"We're about to die!"

I jerk my head to the high-pitched shriek from the back of the plane. "Who said that?" I squeak out.

There's a squawk, then a cry of, "Man overboard!"

I crane my neck to peer past Nolan, checking out the aisle then the galley. I'm not the only one. The other passengers chatter, trying to make heads and tails of the warning.

Everything looks fine, so who's screeching maydays? "What's going on?"

"Get out your life vest," the voice calls out.

Nolan's brow crinkles, and he taps his lip. "Correct me if I'm wrong, but does that sound like a parrot?"

Ohh.

Actually, he's dead right.

Contorting like a rhythmic gymnast in a heist flick, I swivel around and manage to peek over the top of the seat toward the back of the plane.

Turns out the metal crates contain parrots. Inside one of them, a bird with emerald feathers flaps his wings. "That's what she said."

A sapphire bird bleats, "A guy walks into a bar."

I slump into my tiny seat with a groan that slides into laughter. "We're on a flight with the punchline parrots."

Drakkar Noir clears his scratchy throat. "It costs three hundred bucks to fly an animal in its own seat on this airline. Pretty cool, huh? I guess that's how these seats can be so cheap." He pats his cushion. "By the way, I'm Arnie. Those parrots are performing at my comedy club off the Strip tonight if you want to come. The Parrot Club."

That's a little on the nose.

"If you want to come," a bird squawks, echoing Arnie.

"That's what she said," another one says.

"So saucy," I say.

"What time is the show?" Nolan asks.

"Ten p.m."

I glance at Nolan with a face that asks, *Are we going to a parrot comedy night*? The look he fires back says, *Damn straight.*

"We very well might be there," I tell Arnie.

That ought to keep us busy after the party. Lord knows my brain needs busy work when I'm in close confines with my hot, funny, charming best friend, who I still want to kiss like crazy.

* * *

The ruddy man at the rental car kiosk points from Nolan to me and asks, "And are you and your friend . . .?"

The trailing question is annoying. I'm a woman traveling with her best guy friend. So there.

"She's my nanny," Nolan supplies.

I swat the troublemaker.

"I meant babysitter," he says quickly.

I roll my eyes. "I'm actually his billionaire boss," I tell the clerk. "And he's my plucky but undervalued assistant who sends me secret hate letters that I think are sexy."

The man stares at us humorlessly. "I don't care if

you're pen pals or mortal enemies. I only ask because if you're spouses, there's a discount."

"That seems unfair to single people," I point out. "Does this car company discriminate against the unmarried?"

He sighs. He so utterly *can't even* with me. "Lady, I don't have time for bigger battles. I was trying to help you out. If you tell me you're married, I'll give you the discount."

"Someone's a fairy godfather," I say, smile blazing.

"Not really. I get two percent on husband-wife signings."

And he's a hustler too. Gotta respect that, I suppose.

I tilt my chin up at Nolan. "Hey, hubs."

He drapes an arm around me and plants a loud, wet kiss on my cheek. "Hey, wifey."

"Wonderful," the man replies, already typing it in.

Nolan keeps his arm around me as we finish the paperwork. *Settle down, Nancy.* We are simply friends who travel together to cities where we once kissed. And we're even better friends for a discount.

Who wouldn't be?

A deal is hard to resist.

* * *

We cruise down the highway toward the hotel I located on a budget travel site online. When I made our travel plans, I couldn't find any rooms at even the cheapest hotels on the Strip. Apparently, there's a cell phone convention in town, and those phone-makers love the

City of Sin. So, we're headed for a place a couple of miles from the Strip.

Maybe we won't even have rooms near each other. A little distance between us when night falls will surely keep Nancy in check. Maybe.

Nolan drives, following the directions to the Teddy Bear Inn. As he slows the car, the word "vacancy" beckons from the hotel's street sign, though without the "va."

"Get your *cancys* here," I say as Nolan flips on the blinker.

"I've always wanted a *cancy*," he quips, pulling into a parking space.

"You're gonna have everything your heart desires tonight, then," I tease.

Teasing is good.

Teasing is us.

I've so got this.

I sling on my backpack, and we head to the lobby. It's everything the broken-ass sign outside promised. A clogged drain belches near the entryway. Room 102 has a pile of stained towels sitting outside the door. The glass window to the lobby is fogged and cracked.

We are slumming it, but hey, more money for the food offerings for the grandmas.

When I push open the lobby door, a bell announces our arrival, though it's less like a chime, more like a buzz saw. Behind the front desk, a burly man with beady eyes rips off a hunk of a Red Vines and smacks his lips loudly as he chews. "Wazz up?"

"Hey there. We want to check in," Nolan says.

"Cool. Check-in's at three," the man says, pointing to the clock.

"That's in, like, two minutes, man," Nolan says amiably, giving his best *help me out here, bud* grin.

"Exactly." The man takes another bite of the licorice like he's ripping off a chunk of gazelle for dinner and stares at Nolan as he chews.

One hundred twenty seconds later, the man finishes his snack and pushes his Red Vines tub to the other side of the desk. Pasting on a cheery grin, he seems to transform as he says, "And now how can I help you?"

"Surprisingly, we wanted to check in," Nolan says.

"Excellent. What an absolute delight to have you here at the Teddy Bear Inn."

A few minutes later, he hands us each a key to our thirty-nine dollars-a-night rooms. "You two will be right next to each other. And if you need anything, the rooms adjoin too. Just rap on the door next to the TV, and it's almost like a portal to the other room."

"Sounds exactly like a portal. Not almost," I correct.

Oops.

That was the dick in me talking.

"We like to make some things easy," Red Vines man whispers, then gives an exaggerated wink.

Dude, a portal to the man I daydream about isn't making my life easy.

Being in Vegas isn't erasing my wandering thoughts.

Sleeping near Nolan won't settle my pulse.

But we're here for business, so we head down the hall together. "Meet you in an hour to begin our journey," I say to Nolan, then unlock the door to my room, grateful we aren't sharing one since who needs that temptation?

Not me.

Definitely not me.

5

MIDNIGHT ROAD TRIP

Emerson

To say I want to die is an exaggeration, and I am not prone to exaggeration.

But it's with zero hyperbole that, two minutes later, I mutter, "I'm going to die."

With a scarf jammed against my mouth and my overnight bag in hand, I fling myself out of my room. I hold my breath as I pound on Nolan's door.

He bursts out a second later, his carry-on slung on his shoulder, and without consultation, we bolt down the hall, running for our lives.

If we can just make it to the light.

It's close, so close.

Almost there.

I slam a hand on the door, stumble out of the vomitorium motel, and into the afternoon sunlight of the parking lot, gasping.

Palms on knees, I gulp in the fresh air. I fan it into my mouth.

"I'm convinced the prior guest ran an embalming clinic in my room," I tell him, heaving.

"Mine was a secret test lab for how long it takes for food to go bad. The last item they tested was Limburger cheese."

Not to be outdone in the smell arena, I counter with, "Mine also had the distinct aroma of toe jam."

"Mine smelled like belly button lint," he says, determined fucker.

A retch hits the back of my throat and I gag, feeling it down to my toes. "You win. Woman down," I say, waving the white flag since that's a nasty scent.

"We can't stay here tonight," he says.

"Ya think?"

"Seriously. We need to find a room on the Strip, Emerson, even if we have to crack open a piggy bank."

"Agreed, but the Phone Geek Show is in full swing. Maybe we can sleep in the car if we can't find a room. It's better than that," I say, pointing at the putrid Teddy Bear Inn.

But time's a-ticking; we'll have to deal with the room situation later. The Impress Dot and Bette Project, featuring amazing Vegas food, begins now.

It starts at The Cosmopolitan, home to Momofuku and its divine Brussels sprouts. The first order of business is to stop there and snag some goodies to review with the two besties in their home.

Actually, the first order of business is to freshen up, and since I couldn't do it in the Teddy Bear tar pits, I pop into a luxurious ladies' room off the casino floor. A love seat graces a lounge area, and as I reapply lip liner in the mirror, I make an executive decision.

I march out to meet Nolan by the *Wizard of Oz* slot machine and issue my declaration: "It's official. I will sleep in the ladies' room here if I have to."

"Cool. The men's room is pretty sweet too. We can be Cosmopolitan stowaways."

Next up, we climb back into the little red rented Hyundai and head to the nearest 7-Eleven for a review of gourmet pretzels and Slurpees. When we're done, Nolan drives to the other food spots to grab the dishes for our trio of samplers.

Meanwhile, I edit on the go then hit post on our quickie episode. Next, I tackle a hotel search, but I have no luck finding an available room that won't require a new bank loan. "We might be better off just driving back to San Francisco tonight," I suggest after coming up empty.

"Brains and beauty. Let's do a midnight road trip."

"We'll take all the photos."

"For your road trip collection," he says.

In vivid flashes I imagine snapping shots of this trip with Nolan—goofy smiles, cheeky looks, silly poses. I'd put them on the mantel, let him share space with my other collection.

"You know it. And we can review all the convenience stores on the way home," I add.

"You are hardcore, Emerson." He waggles his eyebrows. "And I mean that in all the good ways."

I laugh, shaking my head. "Yeah, I'm not sure hardcore is the compliment you think it is."

As we slow at a light, he shrugs. "Maybe it is."

And maybe it could be.

Like in another world where we weren't besties, where we weren't business partners hanging on by a thread. Maybe then, he'd say we could be together in some way.

Like in the bedroom for one night.

Maybe he'd say he'd help me let loose all my deep, dark fantasies. That he knows them already.

And perhaps I wouldn't mind sharing them with him.

But those what-ifs aren't my reality, so I'm left with this—he's possibly the world's biggest flirt.

Yeah, that's the guy I know so well.

The flirt monster.

* * *

A little later, the back seat is brimming with our offerings. We putter through a cute neighborhood a couple miles away from the hubbub of the Strip, following the robotic GPS voice until we're pulling into the driveway of a stucco house graced by oversized cowboy boot statues on the lawn.

Texas meets Vegas.

Dot and Bette wait for us on the front porch, lounging in rocking chairs, glasses of lemonade in their hands, smiles on their warm faces. Dot wears a red gingham dress. Bette has donned teal gingham.

It is love at first sight.

They are the antidote to Super Saver Squish Me to Pieces Airline. The opposite of The Teddy Bear Smell Chamber of Horror.

My soul feels calm.

It could also be that I've had a long, stressful day. Being back in this city kicks up memories.

Still, as I step out of the car and shut the door, my heart skitters with a crazy sense of hope. A hope I haven't felt this strongly since Nolan said yes to the show more than a year ago.

Maybe I *can* finally turn this into a bona fide online hit. That's what Callie wanted for us back when she asked me to launch *How to Eat a Banana* with her a few years ago. We created the show together for fun, as a little side thing. Slowly, we found an audience. Then, she died, and the show went on hiatus as I went to pieces.

But, thanks to friends and family, I pulled myself together and devised a new plan.

Nolan was back in the States and looking for a gig.

Maybe I could convince him to be my new partner. To start it over.

One chilly fall afternoon, I took him to his favorite mac-and-cheese shop—since the guy just loves that dish —plied him with the Gouda specialty and asked him if he wanted to be my new co-host.

"Want to get the band back together? Only the band would now be you and me?" I asked.

Fork midair, he paused. "You want me to be your second banana?"

I laughed. "No, we'll both be first bananas. Like Callie and I were. Or not. I mean, we didn't even call ourselves bananas. It was just a funny name because there's no way to eat a banana innocently."

He nodded a few times as if deeply considering the offer. "Bananas are *ripe* for innuendo." Another pause, then he sighed contently. "All right. I'm in. When do we start?"

I squealed. "Are you sure? It's that simple?"

"It's that simple."

The next week, we relaunched the show, finding our own sexy shtick, amping up the flirt and the banter since, well, we could.

The show evolved, reflecting our tastes and style. Still, the Web series keeps me close to Callie. Makes her feel alive in a way, since it was her idea in the first place.

I loved working on it with her, and I want her to know I'm taking care of her baby. Even though I've made it my own. I cast my gaze to the blue sky, sending her a wish. *I'm doing this, like you said I would.*

I walk to the porch even though I want to run.

"Hi, Dot. Hi, Bette," I say. "Thank you so much for inviting us here. I'm Emerson." I offer my hand.

"I'm Nolan," my best friend says.

Dot stands first, waves off my palm, then opens her arms wide. "I'm a hugger, sweetie pie. I come from a long line of huggers, and it cannot be stopped. So, forgive me," she says, wrapping strong arms around me.

Yup. *Insta-love, I am in you.* "Nothing to forgive," I say, a little choked up. "I'm a hug monster too."

She lets go. "Then we'll get along fine."

Bette snares me in a tight embrace next. "You look like Audrey Hepburn," she declares when she lets go.

I take that compliment and tuck it in my pocket for when I feel blue. "Thank you."

"And you? Well, hello there, Clark Kent," Bette says to Nolan.

Ever the gentleman, he takes her hand and kisses the knuckles. "Pleased to meet you. If you need anyone to leap a tall building in a single bound, I'm your man."

Bette chuckles, warm and exuberant. "And I do believe I've died and gone to I've-been-charmed heaven."

I'm giddy and alive with possibilities. I run a hand over the ladybug charm. Maybe I do believe in luck. Maybe it's coming our way tonight.

"Come on inside and you can meet Evelyn," Dot says, then drops her voice to a whisper. "Warning though—she's kind of a hard-ass."

"That's what a business manager should be," I say, picturing a stern woman in a pantsuit, protecting her clients like a shark.

Good on Dot and Bette for having a tough-as-nails manager.

Dot swings open the door, then leads us into the living room of a sun-drenched home. The couch is strewn with pillows declaring *Bless this mess or bring me wine to accept it,* and the walls boast sassy inspirational sayings like *Give me the strength to deal with people.*

Yup, I have found my soul mates.

I realize there's a teenager perched in a chair, aimlessly swinging one foot in a black high-top. She's clutching a purple phone that matches the fishnet stockings visible under her ripped jeans. Standard high-schooler attire. "Hey, there," she says, too cool for school.

"Hey. How's it going?" Is she their makeup artist? Her smoky lids are banging. "Nice eyelashes."

"Thanks. Same."

I smile my thanks as the girl flicks her thumb over the screen, then silence hangs between us for a few seconds.

Is she Dot's granddaughter? Her coloring is similar to the Texan's.

"Well, nice to meet you," I say politely, expecting to follow Dot into another room, but when I turn, I bump into her where she stands.

"Oh, sweetie pie," she says, "you need to talk to Evelyn first."

"Anytime," Nolan says with his easy charm. "Let us know when she arrives."

Dot laughs. "You're too cute." Then she points. "That's Evelyn."

Ohhhhh.

"My granddaughter," Dot adds. "She handles the YouTube and all the Twitters."

"Don't forget the tic-tac-toe," Bette chimes.

A groan rolls off the teen. "Bette, please," Evelyn says, her dignity mortally wounded.

"I just like to rile you up. You do your thing, Evelyn," Bette adds with a bye-bye wave.

Evelyn nods at Dot, assuring her, "I'll take care of everything."

Take care of what?

Did we enter a deal with the devil? Are we about to get roofied? Should I run for cover? But Nolan seems chill about the whole thing.

Goth Girl points to the chairs across from her. "Sit, please. I have some items to review." Her tone brooks no argument, and we sit like proper marionettes. "Let's start from the top," she says. "Have you ever had a DUI?"

I shake my head. Nolan does the same. "No," we chime in unison.

"Have you ever been arrested?"

"No," I say emphatically.

Nolan says no as well. Obviously.

"Have you ever posted a shot of yourself guzzling a beer, wine, tequila, or other beverage and looking like a dumbass online?"

My brain quickly cycles back over the last ten years. God, I hope not. "No."

Nolan lifts a hand sheepishly. "I once posted a picture of myself drinking a beer at a baseball game with my buddies," he confesses.

Evelyn nods without giving anything away and seems to make a checkmark on her phone.

"Have you ever said anything inflammatory, derogatory, rude, stupid, idiotic, or insensitive about a marginalized group of people?"

"God, no," I say.

"Of course not," he seconds.

She rattles off a few more feet-to-the-fire questions, then nods a few more times as she takes notes on her phone. I glance at Nolan with a silent *What the hell?* He shrugs an *I'm as surprised as you are*.

Evelyn sets down her phone, steeples her fingers, and stares. Damn, she'd give Jack Donaghy on *30 Rock* a run for his money. The kid is intense.

"Here's the deal. I already ran a background check on the two of you. It looks like everything is solid. You don't have any priors. And a thorough review of your social media indicates that you haven't posted any nudes, any racist or inflammatory remarks, or any douchey comments about anyone."

"You checked out all of that?" Nolan asks. "In twenty-four hours?"

"That's, like, literally my job," she says as if she can't believe anyone wouldn't do the same. "But I did want to confirm a few things." She holds my gaze. "Let me know if these facts are correct. If not, please elaborate, as we like to know who we're working with. First, I see that for the last five years you've lived in an apartment you shared with your twin sister until her death. And now, you live by yourself. Is that true?"

I swallow past the knot of memories in my throat, but words are harder.

"Yes, that's correct," Nolan says, jumping in like a superhero, sensing what I need at this moment.

Evelyn turns to Nolan. "You were in France for two years with an Inés Delacroix. You moved back to San Francisco, worked in a restaurant there, and rented.

Now you've been going back and forth and staying with friends in New York and San Francisco, including your brother. Go Hawks," she says, with a fist pump. "Love them—they used to be in Vegas. Anyway, all of that is correct?"

"Yes," he mumbles.

"What? I didn't hear you."

"That's all accurate," I put in. It's my turn to look out for him as she outlines the ups and downs of his recent years.

"Well, let me just say—living with your brother . . . that is such a great millennial life hack," Evelyn says with admiration.

"Yeah, thanks," Nolan says drily. I can hear his sarcasm, but I know him. Hopefully, she can't tell. "It's my DIY life."

"Perf. You two are all Gucci." She swings her phone to us. "Sign this memorandum saying you won't talk smack about Dot and Bette, and then you can shoot."

Wow. This kid is a shark. "I want you repping me someday," I say as I sign her memo.

"Let us know if you take on more clients," Nolan adds as he signs.

"I will, but let's be honest. I have a lot of calculus homework, so it's probably not going to happen."

"Understandable," I say solemnly.

She points to the hall then returns her attention to her phone. "Oh my God, that's so extra," she says to the screen, and we're done with the sixteen-year-old Great White.

* * *

This is a dream kitchen, and Nolan has a woody for it.

"I want to marry this kitchen," he says of the palace where we've set up the taste test.

"I want to have babies with it," I put in.

"Let me tell you, sweetie pie," Dot says, "this kitchen has seen some action, if you know what I mean." She adds a bawdy wink.

"You're such a bad girl." Bette laughs then smiles for the camera. "Now, did you know it's my favorite time of day, Dot?"

"Bedtime?"

"Try again," Bette says.

"Wine o'clock?" Dot offers.

"Girl, it's taco time."

We spend the next few minutes indulging in the food we brought, finishing with the tacos, then Bette starts in again.

"Now, I have a bone to pick with you, Dot." She shakes a finger at her bestie. "How can you have been my friend for years but never once taken me to Tacos El Gordo?"

"Shame on me. Just shame, shame, shame." Dot lowers her head but quickly snaps it up. "This just means we're going to need regular recs from Nolan and Emerson. These two know where everything good is, from the Brussels sprouts to the egg sandwiches to these divine tacos. Will you two please keep sharing your faves?"

Nolan flashes a panty-melting grin. "You two will always get special treatment," he promises.

And hearts flutter.

"But you know what I really want to try?" Nolan continues. "Those zucchini nachos you were teasing me about. Don't hold out on me now."

Dot slides a tray to us. "Never. You can have everything you want. But, Nolan," she chides, "we have a ladies-first philosophy here."

"But of course," he says, then scoops up a zucchini nacho and offers it to me.

From his hand.

He's feeding me the chip, the fucking ham.

When in Vegas . . .

I part my lips and crunch into it, and my taste buds shimmy. When I finish, I lick my lips. "Look, I know I have a rep for loving stuff, but I just do! This is a double *I'd do it again*. I'm giving it a nine point one."

Our hostesses bump hips. "We got it going on," Bette sings, then flaps her hand at Nolan. "Your turn, bad cop."

He takes a chip, chews, then groans in absolute delight. When he's done, he takes a deep breath, then issues a declaration: "I'm giving this an eight point nine two."

Dot and Bette squeal.

"He hasn't given anything close to a nine in months," I say.

"If you gave us a nine, I would know you were sucking up," Dot says. "So, I like this score a lot."

Maybe we are sucking up a little, but for a good

cause. This is special, the chemistry the four of us have, and I can't help but think YouTube will see it too. We will be hard to beat, and maybe this is it—our chance.

* * *

At their party later, Dot and Bette introduce us to friends and family like we're the special guests. It's heady, and I feel all kinds of floaty. I can't help but admire what Nolan achieved—this last-minute opportunity at a win we need.

That gratitude blooms inside me over the evening, as swing music plays, as guests indulge in cauliflower tater tots and Greek salad skewers, and as conversation flows like the Bellagio Fountains. This night is an unexpected oasis in the middle of all the work-my-ass-off weeks.

It'll end, of course, when we hit the Hyundai to haul our butts across state lines in the middle of the night. But even the prospect of the drive looks brighter than it would have yesterday.

As the party winds down, Dot and Bette tug us down the hallway to a quieter section of the house.

"Listen, cuties," Bette begins, touching my shoulder lightly. "We are so glad you made your way out to Vegas."

"And at the last minute too. We're just so tickled," Dot continues, all the Texas charm dripping in her voice. "We love meeting new friends, and you're good people."

"So, we wanted to thank you in a special way. We

have a little parting gift for y'all." Bette points to the living room. "Evelyn can give it to you."

My cup of gratitude overfloweth. "You ladies are the best." I hug them both. "And I'll edit the video tonight and send it to Evelyn in the morning for approval."

Dot smiles. "I know it'll be fabulous. But you do that, or Evelyn will have my hide." She faux shudders.

"We won't let you incur her wrath," Nolan promises, then does his whole kiss-on-the-top-of-the-hand routine, eliciting giggles and *you're the best*s.

As they return to their guests, Nolan starts toward the living room, but I grab his arm. He's next in the Emerson love fest. "Hey. This was an amazing idea you had, reaching out to them. I have a good feeling about this."

A smile spreads nice and easy on his lush lips. "Yeah?" He sounds so happy, like I've thrilled him with the compliment.

"I do. You found a great opportunity. Is it crazy that I feel we're onto something?"

"I told you we'd get lucky in Vegas," he says, those playful eyes straying to my ladybug charm.

His stare lasts longer than usual. My skin heats under his gaze, my emotions flipping from gratitude to . . . desire.

Ugh.

It's so annoying having a charming, sexy, fun best friend I want to bang.

But I've dealt with it for years.

I've got this.

I reroute to friendship.

But when Nolan pulls his gaze away, dragging a hand through his hair, he looks like he's clearing away his thoughts.

Were they the same thoughts as mine? Is he resetting too?

Oh, shit. Oh, fuck. Oh, my.

That's a little terrifying.

But it doesn't matter. I refuse to obsess over things that won't happen. I can't.

"And now we're getting out of Vegas," I say, focused on the plan, *only* the plan. "We'll need lots of caffeine for our drive. What do you think the gift is? Hot coffee? Chocolate? Kale chips?" I ask as we walk down the hall.

"I'm praying for snacks. We can indulge on our midnight road trip," Nolan says.

We reach the living room, where Evelyn's waiting by the door, empty-handed. Maybe it's not snacks, then.

Evelyn twirls the charm on her phone. "Thanks again for coming. Dot and Bette had such a good time with you, and since they're friends with the women who own The Extravagant, they wanted to get you a suite there tonight. I don't know if you already have a hotel room but—"

"We'll take it," Nolan and I say at the same time.

6

ROLLER COASTER KISS

Nolan

I don't know why people say they remember something like it was yesterday. I don't remember half the details of yesterday. What the hell did I wear when I met Emerson outside her morning TV show gig, or chow down on with Jason after an evening workout, or listen to while I packed my overnight bag?

No clue.

But I have a photographic memory of the way Emerson licked her lips when she finished that veggie burger earlier in the week.

I can picture with crystal clarity the way the black bridesmaid dress she wore to her friend Katie's almost-wedding clung to her chest when she modeled it for me.

And here's another thing.

I've got total recall on that kiss in Vegas. Maybe that

means my dick has an excellent memory. Fine, my dick didn't get a kiss, but he definitely paid attention and filed all the data away in Dick Central Storage, where all the important data is kept.

I'd just returned from France. I've got nothing against that country, but it was a relief to get far, far away from Inés Delacroix. My family had warned me against her. My brother and dad both thought she was bad news.

Spoiler alert—they were right.

That woman was more toxic than a nuclear reactor. Little-known fact—relationships qualify as radioactive when one person is faithful and the other has a couple lovers on the side. Inés had four, so I needed several decontamination showers after returning to the States.

My friends wasted no time urging me to get back out there.

"Now that you've escaped the evil clutches of your ex, it's time to take advantage of your single status again," my friend TJ had said over text. "And that should start in Vegas."

He had a point. Our friends from the Quesadilla Club in college—Dina and Lauren—were getting hitched, so they invited the whole crew to Vegas for the wedding. It seemed like a perfect weekend, a chance to hang out with friends and fellow food lovers. Maybe I'd enjoy a rebound or just enjoy time with my buds. I was cool with whatever, I'd told TJ.

And so I went to Vegas, ready to have a good time before I started a new gig as a sous chef in San Francisco, a respite before I moved in with a bunch of roommates I found online.

The bride and bride hosted about ten of us, giving out chips as wedding favors. The night before the wedding, we broke out the purple ones and hit the blackjack tables at the New York, New York Hotel.

One by one, our friends went bust and decided to hit the roller coaster ride—TJ and Flynn, Dina and Lauren, and the rest of them peeling away from the tables.

But I was playing well, so I stayed in the casino, Emerson by my side. I was up by five hundred dollars and contemplating staying in, flipping the chip between my fingers, when Emerson rubbed her hands on her thighs.

Her nervous tell.

She'd done it in college when she was stressed about a test.

She did it when she was worried about her sister's medical appointments.

My attention shot away from the card game. "What's wrong? Are you okay?"

She drew a shuddery breath, her eyes straying toward where our friends had disappeared. "I have to tell you something."

"Fire away," I'd said, then left the table, cashing out.

"I hate roller coasters," she blurted out, rubbing her palm on her jeans again.

I pressed my hand on top of hers and squeezed. "You don't have to go, then," I said gently. "We'll meet them when they get off."

But Emerson seemed to shuck off her anxiety with a

crisp nod. "No, I want to do it. Callie used to love them. When we were kids, we used to ride them together, and she can't ride them anymore. Her heart, and all. She wanted me to ride this on my trip."

I was confused. "But she knows you hate them?"

"Yes. But here's the thing: I used to love them too. Then last summer, I read a news article about a roller coaster that got stuck upside down for five minutes. I told John about it, and he proceeded to tell me every single terrible thing that had ever happened at amusement parks, chapter and verse. He had the facts at his fingertips."

I sneered at the mention of her ex, Useless Fact Freddie. "That guy was a fucking tool. He was incapable of having fun. He had to tell you the amount of fat in every food, the risk of slipping in the shower, and the chances of falling out of a roller coaster."

"Yes, I believe he's what's known as a buzzkill. Anyway, point being, Callie and I recently decided to do this thing where we face our fears. And she already did hers. Ergo . . ."

"It's your turn?"

"Yup, and she killed it at hers. Here's a pic." Emerson whipped out her phone, slid her thumb across the screen, and showed me a shot of her and her sister . . . holding a pink, fleshy, veiny, foot-long, super-powered rabbit toy.

"Yeah, that scares the fuck out of me too," I said, taking in the super-size schlong. "You could smack someone in the face and take out an eye."

She snorted. "Yes, that was the fear she had to get over. Losing an eye," she deadpanned.

I studied the pic. "Was your sister scared of a dildo?"

Shaking her head, Emerson stuffed the phone in her back pocket. "No. Of buying one. She'd never gone to a sex toy shop before. So, I took her to my favorite, where I get all my toys." Emerson smiled and set her hand on her heart, beaming at her sister's accomplishment—a complete contrast to the pinball game my brain was playing, buzzers whirring, lights flashing because . . . *sex toys*. "And I swear, I've never been so proud of her." She pretended to choke up. "She was a big girl, asking all sorts of questions about the vibe's ability to deliver toe-curling Os."

"Wow. That's inspiring," I said drily, mostly to keep from asking a litany of questions that shot up unexpectedly in my head. *What kind of toy do you like?* and *Does it make you shake all over in pleasure, grab the sheets, and scream my name?*

"And now it's my turn to face my fears," she said. "But I need help."

Her eyes implored me, but I couldn't resist. "You sure you don't need to run another sex toy errand?"

A laugh fell from her pretty lips. What did those lips look like when she used her favorite toy?

"Roller coasters first. Sex toys another time," she said, then squared her shoulders. "Will you ride with me?"

Before I could even fashion an answer, my brain pinged with questions: Had I always been attracted to her? Had I never realized it till we talked about sex toys? Or had I never admitted it to myself?

I didn't have the answers. But I knew she'd asked for help, and that meant it was friend time, not the horn-dog hour.

"Yes. I will."

We marched to the roller coaster and tucked our phones and my glasses into a locker. As we moved through the line, I psyched her up like a coach working with a boxer. I rubbed her shoulders, said *you can do this,* and reassured her that we'd have fun like she did when she was younger.

Then, we reached the front of the line.

"After you," I said, a proper gentleman as I gestured to the cars.

She stepped in, and I joined her. The seat belts came down, snapping us in place.

"Have I ever told you my recipe for pancakes?" I asked.

"No," she said, tilting her head, curious.

As the car lurched away from the platform, I told her precisely how I made amazing blueberry pancakes. As it chugged up the first killer hill, she reached for my hand and clasped my palm, then threaded her fingers with mine. Tight, and a little sexy too. She stroked the top of my hand while sliding her fingers in and out of mine.

It was . . . weirdly erotic.

While talking about pancakes in the chilly Vegas night air, we rose above the city, and she turned me on as I settled her down.

When we neared the top, she stroked faster and I

talked quieter. The moment was wildly arousing in ways I never expected, like she was seducing me with her fingers.

New thoughts raced through my head.

She's sexy.

She's fun.

She's the friend I want to fuck.

When we shot downhill, she screamed her lungs out —"Oh my fucking God" style, saying my name over and over again.

"Oh God, Nolan, oh God, Nolan, oh God, Nolan."

My adrenaline shot through the roof from the roller coaster, the speed, the thrill. Her hair whipped her cheeks. Her face flushed red. She screamed my name like she was coming.

Every desire I'd suppressed about Emerson rose from the depths of a sea of dirty thoughts, burst through the surface, and reared up like Poseidon the Giant Prick.

That ride unlocked the sea monster of lust in my brain.

Thanks, thrill ride.

The roller coaster slowed and finally stopped, and we jumped off. Emerson turned, ecstatic and victorious, and flung her arms around me. "I could kiss you."

I was too twisted in my own filthy mind to do anything but flash her a dopamine-charged grin. "I won't stop you."

Letting go of my shoulders, she grabbed my face and pressed a buzzy, heady kiss to my lips.

Just a thank-you kiss. I knew that. It was as chaste as

a kiss on the lips could be. But I craved more, so before she could step away, I inched closer, hand on her face, holding her jaw. "Just one more kiss," I whispered.

Her chin tilted up like I'd said the perfect thing. "Okay," she said, all breathy and full of want.

We kissed once again. It was no longer an exuberant *oh my God* kiss. It was slow and sweet, with a question in it. It was a *do you feel it too?* kiss.

I felt it.

She sure as hell seemed to feel it.

It was an unexpected coda to the wilder kiss. An encore that said *Yes, I want to kiss you again.*

We stopped a few seconds later, blinking, breathing fast. She swept her hand along her hair, still messed up from the ride. "Wow."

"Yeah. Wow."

But there was no time to bask in the moment. The other riders had filed off, and we had a picture to pick up at the photo booth and then friends waiting.

Once we grabbed the image, we found our group in the concourse of the hotel. We joined Dina, Lauren, TJ, Flynn, and the others, and went to a dance club.

We didn't dissect the kiss. Maybe because it was too short. Or maybe because it was long enough to matter. And if it mattered, it was a risk. One that could tip us out of the friend zone.

Later that night, as the wedding party fanned out to our rooms, Emerson set a hand on my arm then showed me the pic of us from the ride. We looked joyful. "Thank you for going with me. You're my best friend. Well, best friend who's not my sister."

"I know, Em," I said. "I know."

She frowned. "Shit, sorry. I don't mean to qualify it."

But I got it completely. "I don't feel second best. You can't replace a twin."

She smiled sadly. She knew what was coming sooner rather than later with her sister. "That's why this means the world to me—like you do."

I understood her one hundred percent. Our friendship mattered more than a kiss. We couldn't do that again.

Made sense, really. I was a mess from Inés, and she'd been fucked over by guys she'd dated. Plus, her focus was on her sister, and I didn't want to lose a friend either.

It was just a roller-coaster-fueled kiss, and it wouldn't happen again.

* * *

So, here we are in the same city. We're still best friends, but we're also a helluva lot more. Best friends and business partners. Double whammy.

But, hey, if we avoid roller coasters, it won't be a problem. The Extravagant doesn't have one, so we'll be fine. Just fine.

We check into the hotel without any fuss, Emerson handing over a credit card for incidentals as we gawk at the jewel-themed opulence in the lobby. When the clerk gives us two key cards, I'm poised to walk away.

Emerson spins back to look at the clerk. "Oops. Meant to ask. Are there two queens? A king?"

The woman at the desk glances down at the monitor then flashes a grin. "A king and a large pull-out sofa. Will that work for you?

"Perfect," she says.

And it is perfect. There's room for two in this hotel suite.

We head to the elevators. "Inquiring minds want to know—do you want to go to The Parrot Club?" she asks.

It takes me a few seconds to register her meaning—the comedy club with the talking birds. But I shake my head. "Nah, let's just edit the episode and hit the hay."

She doesn't answer right away. She takes a few seconds. "Excellent plan."

We step into the elevator and head upstairs. The ride lasts forever. I study the posters, reading one about the room amenities, advertising them as *fully equipped.*

Equipped for what?

But I don't ask because another question blasts across all my gray matter: Is she thinking of roller coaster kisses?

On the twelfth floor, we walk together into a luxury hotel room, and it feels like we're at the first drop on an amusement park ride.

7

BATHROBES WILL SAVE ME

Emerson

This is not the Teddy Bear Inn.

This room is an advertisement for a Vegas getaway weekend. It's the setting for City of Sin fantasies.

Just look at the dreamy blue lights glowing along the floorboards. Just listen to the soft, sultry music piping into the sumptuous suite.

And check *that* out—the decadent view as lights from The Invitation across the street flash in the floor-to-ceiling window of this suite. They blink *RSVP tonight*.

The plush sapphire-colored carpet hugs my shoes and reminds me to remove those dirty little fuckers.

I kick off my ankle boots as the cool of the air conditioning wraps around us. "Are you sure we're allowed to stay here?" I joke. "Or will they realize we don't belong and toss out all the riffraff?"

Nolan brings his finger to his lips. "Shh. If you don't tell anyone we don't belong, I won't either."

"It's a deal," I say as Nolan toes off his shoes too, then sets down his bag. I put mine on the floor, taking a moment to drink in the rest of the suite.

A cushy purple couch commands center stage in the living room area, along with a glass table and a sleek bar with an ice bucket behind it.

And there's probably a bed around the corner. I mean, duh. All hotel rooms have beds.

Still, my palms sweat at the thought.

Which is silly.

Nolan has crashed many a time at my place and slept on my couch after late-night planning sessions.

Since this hotel suite has a sofa, we're not going to share a bed, so why does the prospect of setting my eyes on a regular old hotel mattress unleash a flurry of tingles down my spine?

I can handle a bed.

No big deal.

I rub my palms on my jeans, trying to erase the rush of anxiety as I pad past the couch, around the corner, and—

Holy mother of sex beds.

Does anyone ever sleep in this bed? It's like the hotelier said to the interior designer: *give me a bed for banging.*

And the designer said: *at your sexy service.*

The cover is red.

The pillows are white.

The headboard is a silvery, padded thingie, perfect

for slamming your palms against when you're riding a hot guy's face.

Whoa.

What the hell was that, Nancy?

Must banish my libido to the timeout chair.

This is just an ordinary bed. In a standard hotel room. I've slept in beds before. Plus, Nolan and I will work tonight. This is a work trip, after all. We'll focus on the show that's poised to take off.

I won't focus on my overactive imagination that wants to straddle Nolan and ride him cowboy. Ride him cowgirl. Ride him till the cows come home.

Wait, wrong analogy.

I'll get on my horse and trot away. Yup, that's more like it.

I wheel around and hook my thumb toward the couch, so I can get as far away from the rodeo bed as possible. "I'm going to grab my laptop and edit the video. You can do the socials."

Nolan leans against the entrance to the bedroom. "Mind if I shower first? Don't know about you, but I kinda can't resist a hot hotel shower."

The steed I rode off on bucks. Whoa, Nellie.

"Shower? Like without clothes? Now?" I squeak.

Nolan tilts his head, studies me like an oddity in a curio shop. And I am. "Usually I shower naked," he says, drawing it out. "But hey, I can try it with clothes on if that's your recommendation. Is that what you're saying? I should stand under the hot water in my shirt and jeans?" He plucks at his Smiths T-shirt.

Giving a careless shrug, I try to play it cool. "I mean, probably clothes-free is best, if I'm being picky."

"Cool. Will try it that way. Naked and all."

"And I'll edit," I say.

With a laugh, he says, "Yes, you mentioned your editing plans."

Well, I meant it, clearly. I will edit and not think of you in your birthday suit, showering. I will not picture joining you. I will not imagine asking you to bite me, bruise me, leave marks.

"The sooner I edit, the sooner we can show our video to Evelyn and then submit it to YouTube for the contest," I say, focusing so damn intently on our goals.

Our *business* goals.

And *business* partners don't share beds. "I'll sleep on the couch," I blurt.

Or maybe I croak it. I'm a frog, clearly. A horny toad.

"No, I'll sleep on the couch, Em," Nolan says, his lips curving into a grin. "But are you okay? You seem kind of . . . hyper."

"Me? Hyper?" My pitch hits glockenspiel range.

"Just a little."

I've got to slice that notion off at the knees. "I'm good. I'm great. Just excited. I want to do a good job on the video. I want it to be amazing. I always edit best right after we shoot, and this room is super conducive to work so . . ."

I'm ridiculous. A shower is just a shower. A room is just a room.

We're friends. Partners. Dreamers.

But we won't be lovers.

I draw a big breath and shoo him away. “Go. Shower. Indulge. Use their fancy bodywash. I bet they have big, fluffy bathrobes too.”

“God, I hope so,” he says drily as he grabs his bag. “There’s nothing I love more than a robe.” Nolan heads to the bathroom and I hear him groan from a room away. “Emerson, this bathroom’s fucking heaven. You’ll want to spend the night in it.”

I smile like a pageant girl with Vaseline-slicked teeth. Yup. This is us. Buddies sharing a suite.

Just like we share a show.

Once the door to the bathroom clicks shut, I dive onto the couch, bury my face in a pillow, and scream.

Then, I get my act together and call for help.

Sitting up, I grab my phone and tap out a quick message to Katie.

Emerson: Random question. On a scale of one to ten, how dangerous is it to share a hotel room with the guy you work with?

Katie: I feel like this might be a trick question.

Emerson: So the answer is . . . not dangerous at all. Cool. I’ll just carry on.

. . .

Katie: I'm going out on a limb here . . . but does this mean you and your hottie co-host with the cute glasses and the charm and the sex eyes and the tight T-shirts are shacking up tonight?

Emerson: You're so mean. Thanks for mentioning he's cute and bangable. Also, we're *just* sharing a room.

Katie: Ah, is this where I tell you *stay strong, girl, in the face of the bangable guy*?

Emerson: Yes! But I'll be fine. There's nothing to stay strong about. He's given me no reason to think he wants to do the hotel bed horizontal shimmy-shimmy, bang-bang . . . So really, I just needed to put the hypothetical sex question out there for you to dismiss and then send it packing for the night.

Katie: So that was a dismiss-the-hypothetical-possibility-of-sex text?

Emerson: And it worked! Yay! I'm no longer sex-crazed.

Katie: Miracles happen!

. . .

Closing the thread, I turn down the music in the suite and get to work as the patter of hot water fills my head.

Nolan's naked a wall away.

Nolan's hands are sliding down his trim belly.

Nolan's tipping his head back under the stream.

"Gah!" I need to check myself into a perv-no-more rehab center. "Focus, girl. Just focus."

And with a deep, soldiering breath, I manage the Herculean task.

I blot out the sound of the shower and I edit the hell out of the video, working my ass off instead of picturing his naked one.

Until he strides out fifteen minutes later, a towel wrapped around his waist, his dark hair slicked back and wet, his black glasses on.

I look up. My jaw tries to come unhinged when a droplet of water sails slowly down his trim chest, heading straight for his happy trail. My tongue is jealous of the droplet.

"Whew, it's a sauna in there," he says, waving a toned arm toward the bathroom.

That arm.

His happy trail.

My hormones.

I ache so badly that I need an ice pack between my goddamn legs. "Cool," I mutter, then with iron will, I return my eyes to the screen.

There. I did it.

For now.

* * *

Nolan declares the video a work of brilliance, and I send it to Evelyn, set the laptop on the bed, then hit the shower myself. Once I'm out, I implement my plan of libido attack to make it through the night.

Wrapping myself in a thick, fluffy bathrobe, I march into the living room, presenting the other oversized robe to Nolan. He's changed into a T-shirt and basketball shorts.

"It's bathrobe time." I waggle it in front of him. "Do it."

He flubs his lips, then shrugs. "When in Vegas."

"I have one more thing for us," I say. "A little surprise."

His hazel eyes twinkle with delight. "I love surprises."

I head to my bag and grab two packaged facial masks, grateful I bought an extra one when they were on sale at CVS the other week.

"Want to do a face mask with me?"

He arches a brow. "A face mask?"

"They're fun. These are grapefruit. Have you ever done one?"

"No."

"Self-care for the win. Let's do it." Because there is nothing sexy about goop on your face.

Face masks paired with oversized terry-cloth robes are proven lady-boner killers. No one has ever wanted to smash her face against her friend's when he was wearing a face mask. I am brilliant on a scale of one to Einstein.

"I'm game," Nolan says. That is one of the things I love about him. His easy attitude. His laidback style. His charm.

I mean, that's what I love about him *as a friend*. I am only thinking friendly thoughts as he sheds his shirt and dons his robe.

We head into the bathroom, and five minutes later, his stupidly handsome face is covered in slippery pink goop, and I am a genius.

"Admit it. I look like a gumball," he says, peering closely in the mirror.

Yup. Friendship talk only. "And I am a stick of cotton candy," I say. "Now we leave these on for fifteen minutes."

Nolan tips his head to the bedroom. "Want to watch those how-to-make-jam videos?"

Yes! How-to videos, face masks, and friendship rituals. We change rooms and he flops on the bed next to the laptop.

The sex bed.

No big deal, no big deal, no big deal.

I settle in next to him, near but not too close, and flick open the screen.

A notification pops up—a beautiful, tempting envelope icon with Evelyn's name. "Open it," I whisper reverently.

Her reply is short and sweet—*This is a go! Can we post it tonight so their subs get it in the morning?*

Nolan points at the screen in wild excitement. "Yes. The gods of the home page will love this."

I love this. "Tell her yes. I'm shaking too much to reply."

"I got your back." He taps at the keyboard, then uploads the video too.

But I'm still shaking. Everything feels possible. I picture my bills. The student loans. The amount I owe. The amount I wasn't supposed to owe.

I think of the chance this partnership represents and I can't stop trembling with excitement.

"Breathe, Emerson. Breathe. It's going to be great," Nolan says softly, squeezing my shoulder.

"It is," I say, choosing to believe.

And when I do, the nerves slink away.

We watch a jam video, debating whether we want to make a strawberry one at some point. Things seem right between us again, like the reset worked. The hotel room didn't win.

I lift a hand and touch the stiff mask on my face. "Want to do the *face mask crack*? My friend Jo and I do it when we face mask on FaceTime."

"That's a thing? Face masks on FaceTime?"

"It's so a thing." I grab the arm of his robe and tug. "C'mon. We have to do it in front of the mirror."

Nolan swings his legs out of bed, and we take our spots in front of the double sinks, smiling big and crazy so our pink peels can crack.

I laugh. He laughs. We are so fine.

As he scrubs off his mask, I do the same.

When I'm done, I pat my face with a towel and

return to the bed. Nolan follows me there and sets a hand on his cheek. "Do I look fabulous?"

"So fierce," I agree, then we settle in and pick a show to chill out to—*That's What She Said.* Quirky rom coms are my jam. His too.

He scoots a little closer to me, maybe to see the screen better. As he inches over, the space between us halves. Wait, quarters. It's the size of one banana.

You could fit a banana between us. That's all that separates me from the man in this bed.

What if we closed the distance the rest of the way?

His clean scent fills my head, making me wonder about those what-ifs.

Nolan straightens his shoulders and stares at my face. "Hold on."

I hit pause on the show, but not my imagination. "What is it?" I ask, breathy at the way his eyes study me so intensely.

"You have a spot here you missed." He tugs his bathrobe cuff down closer to his wrist, which loosens the belt tie a notch, then raises his arm and scrubs at my cheek with the cloth.

"Almost gone," he says, then wets the tip of his finger and dusts it along my jawline.

Goose bumps sweep up my skin.

Nolan rubs a little more, stroking my jaw. My breath catches. I swallow around the knot of longing, trying desperately to hide my arousal.

From the slide of his finger on my face.

From the nearness of his lips.

From the warmth of his touch.

From that exposed skin as my eyes drift down to the V of his chest. I want to put my mouth on his skin, want to bite him and kiss away the ache.

Screw face masks. Forget robes.

I wave the white flag.

"Almost gone," he whispers, brushing my face, stirring up years of unchecked emotions, lust, desire.

I am overcome.

Lifting my hand, I touch his chest, my palm against his skin igniting a flare of heat in my belly. Slowly, because this is a turning point, I look up, unsure what I'll see but certain what I want.

I search his face for an answer to my first move. Those hazel eyes shimmer with need.

"Can I kiss you?" Nolan asks.

"Do it. *Please*," I whisper.

And he RSVPs tonight.

8

FULLY EQUIPPED TURNDOWN SERVICE

Nolan

There's this idea about certain moments in life. That we don't have any choice sometimes. That some sort of cosmic force compels us into action. People often use this idea of "it just happened" to justify why they do something in the heat of the moment.

It's the idea of temporary insanity. Or a temporary explosion of lust. But at the end of the day or at the start of the night, a choice is just that.

A choice.

You make it, and sometimes you do it with no regard for the consequences.

That's me right now.

My hand cups Emerson's jaw, and I'm fully aware of the what-could-go-wrongs, the what-may-implodes.

I just don't give a shit. My want is stronger. I want to kiss her more than I want all the other things in my life.

So, I kiss her.

It's quiet in the room, with only the ambient noise of a hotel. The low hum of air conditioning. The faint honks from traffic down below. And the *thump, thump, thump* of desire pounding through my body as I take her mouth with mine.

We kiss with the growing urgency of a first kiss. True, it's not our first. But it's our only kiss *like this.*

In bed.

With nothing to hold us back.

Lips slide. Breath mingles. Hands get in on the action. With my thumb, I trace lines along her cheek and chin, mapping the shape of her face with my fingers. I let my senses flood with the taste and feel of Emerson, like I'm savoring a glass of wine, its flavors filling my mind.

The faint hint of cinnamon from her toothpaste. The lingering scent of grapefruit from that face mask. Her clean, showery smell.

Most of all, the taste of her hunger.

It radiates off her.

It comes in the soft murmurs she makes. In the pressure of her lips. In the eager exploration of her tongue as she kicks the kiss up a notch, deepening it, like she wants to know exactly what this kiss could be.

It's a whole-body kiss, one I feel in my shoulders, in my stomach, in my fucking balls.

I want to remember every second of this. I want to

recall this intoxicating kiss the next day and the next and the next.

But all moments break apart, a kaleidoscope shifting into another scene.

I pay a visit to her neck, kissing down, down, down to the hollow of her throat, where I press an open-mouthed caress to her soft skin, then a lick.

A sexy groan lands on my ears, and I charge on. Kissing harder.

Emerson ropes her hand around my head, jerking me close as a throaty moan falls from her lips, the faint whimper of the word *more.* She's barely audible. Maybe neither one of us wants to break this moment with too many words.

Good. Because I don't want to analyze this choice. I just want to live in it. Deal with what it means tomorrow.

Since tonight I'm going to fuck my best friend.

That's the way I kiss her.

Like I'm listening to the command of *more.*

I kiss her with every intention of wringing a sheet-grabbing, toe-curling orgasm from her this evening.

My hands move at a determined pace, unknotting the tie of her robe, but then I stop. Look up. "Is this okay?"

Her eyes are hazy with desire. "Very okay," she says, then holds up a finger. "But . . ."

I stop, wondering what's to come. She reaches for my glasses, slides them off my face, then tilts her head. "But maybe like this?"

It comes out so flirty, like the Emerson I know. But

there's also another side of Emerson I desperately want to experience.

Emerson after dark.

"Thanks for helping out a guy with glasses," I say as she sets them on the nightstand.

"Anytime. Have I mentioned how sexy they are?"

I laugh as I undo the tie on her robe, spread the fabric open, then groan in frustration. "No, you haven't, but what the hell, Emerson?"

Her eyes pop. "What the hell, what? Don't you dare say we're stopping."

"God, no. But I was hoping you'd be naked under the robe. You're wearing a bra and panties, dammit."

She laughs. "Conveniently, they're removable."

"Very convenient." I run my hand along her sides, savoring the soft feel of her skin against my palms. I'll get to her clothes soon enough. Right now, I want to touch her all over.

But she seems eager to strip, since she loops her hands behind her back, reaching to undo her bra.

I shake my head, stop her with one hand. Her green eyes darken when my fingers circle her wrist.

Ahhh.

That's a clue.

And it gives me an idea. I squeeze harder, pressing my thumb into her skin.

Her lips part, and the sound that comes from her mouth is all new, and dirtier. A sexy, greedy *yes.*

A little pressure, a little hurt gets her going. "Let me undress you," I say.

Her breath hitches, and she nods. "Be my guest." She

lets her hands fall to the mattress, waiting for me to take over.

I unhook her bra, then shove off the bulky terry-cloth robe. She helps me along, wiggles out of it, pushing both items to the floor. Standing, I shed my robe too.

"I love robes now," I tease, admiring her exposed skin, deliciously pale with freckles coasting along the top of her breasts. Her rosy, pert nipples stand to attention.

"Hello there, beauties," I say to her tits, then I straddle her and bury my face where it belongs.

In the valley of her breasts.

As I lavish her with kisses, the mood shifts once more, tightening, intensifying. It's the climb of the roller coaster, and we're cranking higher and higher. She's arching her back, gasping, then gasping louder when I bite down on a breast, drag my teeth over a nipple.

"Oh God, yes," she murmurs, writhing under me.

I'm learning so many delicious secrets about my friend. Emerson likes it a little rough. A bit hard.

I roll the tip of my tongue along the nipple of her right breast, then her left. Her hands grab at my head, clutching. She grips me harder and tighter. Her moans are shameless.

And I *could* say I have no choice but to keep going.

But really, I'm fully exercising this choice to bite her nipples, to kiss her belly, to nip at her hips.

Then to strip her down to nothing as I tug off her black panties and admire the view.

Wet. Glistening. Pink.

"Look at you," I say, a rumble in my throat. "Just fucking look at you."

She seems to revel in the moment, bask in my dirty gaze as I roam my eyes up and down her naked body, imprinting in my mind the curves and dips, the shape of her, then the shivers that spread along her flesh as I touch her legs.

I rub my thumb along her hip, tracing the outline of a ladybug tattoo. "I didn't know you had *this*," I whisper, then dip my face to the black and red ink.

Kissing her there.

"Yessss," she murmurs.

I lick the outline of it, bite her hip.

She arches her pelvis, and pushes up on her elbows, her eyes straying to my briefs. "Interesting fashion choice," she says, regarding the red boxer briefs with pink flamingos on them.

"Do you really want to talk about fashion right now?" I counter.

"You have flamingos on your underwear. I both want to talk about them and rip them off."

I flop to my back and play with the waistband, teasing. "Pick door number two. Now. Fucking now."

She climbs over me, grabs at my waistband, but then stops. Her head drops to my chest, her chestnut hair spilling across my pecs as she moans in frustration. "Condom. I don't have one with me. It's been a while," she mutters.

I push my head into the pillow and groan too. But then, I man up. "I'll go downstairs and get one."

Unless . . . I glance at the nightstand. "This hotel did say the rooms are fully equipped."

Her green eyes sparkle. "Please let it be equipped for safe sex."

With a laugh and a hope, I stretch an arm to the drawer, slide it open, and reach inside.

Yes! The feel of foil makes my dick even harder. "*That* is turndown service."

"And now I will open that door," she says, then hooks her thumbs into the waistband of my boxer briefs and slides them down, moving along my body as she strips me.

My cock gives her a one-eyed salute.

She draws a sharp breath, then she nibbles on the corner of her lips. Once more, the mood tilts. She crawls back up my body, straddles me again, and grips my dick.

Everything else vanishes into the Vegas night. All the choices. All the consequences. All the what-ifs.

They distill down to the feel of her hand on me. The heat in her eyes. The way I can't stop looking at her as she strokes me.

I still her moves then wrap my arm around her waist and slide her down to the mattress so her back is against those soft hotel sheets and she's spread out before me, a naked masterpiece to admire. "Want to look at you. Touch you. Fuck you like this," I say as I kneel between her legs, slide my hands down her thighs, press them wide open. I dig my thumbs into her flesh, my short nails scratching her skin.

Her back bows, and she pushes the side of her face into the pillow like she's hiding her moan.

I grab her jaw, pull her face back so she's looking at me. "Let me see you."

"Okay," she murmurs, her expression one of frenzied need.

Yeah, sometimes you just give in. Because you're thirty years old. Because you've thought about fucking her more times than you want to admit. Because you're wildly attracted to your best friend.

Because there are so many reasons not to, but you're two adults who want each other. That's sometimes the only reason that counts.

I roll on the condom, rub the head of my cock against her wetness, then slowly, deliciously, push inside. She breathes out, tenses, then gives me a nod to keep going. I sink in, filling her all the way, pushing her knees up toward her chest, my pecs a few inches from her tits. She reaches for me, hands curling over my shoulders, and lifts her face toward mine, asking for a kiss.

And it's the best kind of kiss, and the best kind of sex.

It's kissing and fucking. Fucking and kissing.

Finding that rhythm. Moving with the other person.

I follow her cues. Listen to the sound of her breathing. Watch her face. She's loud—surprisingly so. I guess I thought she was just flirty for fun, just dirty for show.

But that mouth becomes something else in bed, a sort of unfettered truth as her fingers race through my hair, tugging.

She cries out.

Moans.

Begs.

It's incredible, and I fuck her harder. One hand slides down to her ass and I grip her flesh. "You like that?"

"I do," she rasps out.

I grab and knead, maybe leaving marks. She urges me on with those gorgeous moans.

I dip my face to her neck, bite down on her collarbone. A long *ohhh* spills from her lips as she grabs my ass, jerks me deeper, and whispers in my ear, "I'm close."

I push up on my elbows. "How can I get you there?"

"Let me be on top."

Fifteen seconds later, we've maneuvered around.

She's on top of me, riding me. Playing with herself and losing her mind.

I squeeze her tits, pinch her nipples, and stare. Just stare shamelessly at the woman riding my cock, parting her lips, and then breaking apart.

She calls out my name like she did that night on the roller coaster, her face flushed pink, her hair wild.

But it's better. So much better. All real, all true.

I suppose this is the moment when there is no choice. I literally have no choice but to follow her into the land of orgasmic bliss.

9

MORNING PEACOCK RECKONING

Emerson

The thing about fantasies is they end when you're done.

As in *done with the deed.*

While I've pictured sex with Nolan countless times, I've never thought about the morning after. There's been no need to. The director of my late-night bedroom dreams was always focused on the between-the-sheets action sequence and didn't bother to script out the following day.

The sunrise scene in my screenplay opens on a blank page. I'm trying to figure out my dialogue and my action.

What comes after the money shot?

Well, in porn they don't show you, but you gotta clean up the mess. In real life, the same applies, and it's called the reckoning.

As blinding sunlight blares through the window the next morning, I lie awake in the cushy hotel bed, eyes wide open, wondering what the hell to say when Nolan rouses.

I've been lying here for thirty-four minutes.

Thinking.

With a sigh, I stare into the doorway to the living room. I want to get out of bed, check my phone, do some work. But what if that wakes him? What would we say about last night?

Reckonings involve mouths and talking.

Also, weirdness.

The morning after you sleep with your best-friend-turned-business-partner can't be anything but weird.

Maybe I don't need a script to tell me there'll be inevitable lines like: *Thanks for the O. Want some pancakes?* Or *That was cool, but you don't expect that to happen again, right? Since I have a date with a hot new Tinder hookup.*

Or worse . . . nothing.

My stomach flip-flops. But what did I expect? We're not going to become a thing. Time to put the genie back in the bottle so we can stay friends and move forward as business partners.

No matter how weird it'll be. That's the price to pay for last night's fun.

And was it ever fun . . . and good . . . really good . . . and kind of amazing. I shift around, unwilling to leave the warm bed quite yet. Plus, the view. With my head propped on my elbow, I savor the scene a little longer. The deepest sleeper in all the land, Nolan's still conked out, face-planted on his pillow, dark hair sticking up in all directions.

My heart glows a little because he's so damn cute.

And sexy.

I lift a hand reflexively, wanting to run it down his smooth back, to learn how his golden, sun-kissed skin feels in the morning light. To discover if that little scratch I left on the side of his neck smarts. If I can soothe it with a soft kiss.

To ask, too, if he's bothered by all the biting, scratching, clawing.

Except I know the answer, how much he was into it. A spark wiggles down my belly, a treacherous and beautiful reminder of how good it felt to tangle our bodies together.

Feelings kick around in me, and I'm an electrified bundle of nerves again. I long to hear gravelly morning-after words like *That was so good, You're incredible,* and *Did it feel that good for you too?*

Risky feelings.

I glance at the clock again. I've been here for forty-one minutes now, which means only three hours till our flight. Prepping to go will keep me busy and help us avoid a long, drawn-out reckoning.

Quietly, I pad to the bathroom, snick the door shut, and make quick work of getting ready. I brush my teeth, enjoy a quick shower, and get dressed while he's still asleep.

I head to the living room, grab my phone from where I left it last night, and take it off do not disturb.

My home screen is littered with notifications.

An email from my parents; the preview says *That's our girl!*

A text from Jo in New York, saying, *Can I say I knew you when? So proud of you!*

Is this happening? I click on the next icon. The pane reveals a note from Hayes, our talent agent. *Thanks for making my life easier. All those meetings I had about you guys are going to get a lot more interesting!*

My skin prickles.

I shudder with want.

There's one more email to click open. A message from YouTube itself blinks in the corner of my screen. It's like I've been summoned to the top of Mount Olympus, and I walk in, reverently, head bowed, dropping to one knee in supplication at Zeus's feet. *I am at your service.*

I swipe it open, my heart in my throat as I read.

Dear Nolan and Emerson,

Congratulations! Your How to Eat a Banana collaboration with Dot and Bette is a shining example of creativity among two top partners. We're so pleased to feature you on the home page. Please note, this is a rolling contest with new entries accepted from other creators throughout the dates of the competition. You are ineligible to enter again, but we did want to congratulate you on being the first winners in the collaboration series.

YouTube

. . .

I inhale sharply. Hold the breath. Shake my head. Close my eyes. Open them.

I read the note one more time to make sure it's not a joke and check the email address too. Yes, it truly is from the site.

Then I exhale.

My chest handsprings.

I click to the home page of the world's biggest video site. A moment later, I slap my palm over my gaping mouth.

That's me.

That's *us.*

Those are our new friends.

I stay frozen for long seconds, gulping in air, trying to adjust to this new reality.

Then I let it hit me blissfully in the chest. I jump. I gasp. I scream. "NOLAN!"

There's a rustle of covers and a quick wake-up yawn. "What? What's going on?"

I rush into the bedroom as Nolan tumbles out of bed, morning wood tenting his flamingo boxers.

Big time.

Like, my eyes can't stop eating up the view.

That good morning bulge—straight out and proud—is thoroughly distracting. *Lick my lips as my lady parts purr* distracting.

Must resist.

Must stay strong.

Why am I here? Right. The phone!

I waggle it at him, this proof that we accomplished a crazy, wild goal that seemed out of reach. We went for a

Hail Mary pass and scored a touchdown to win the game.

"Home page. Home page, home page, home page, home page, home page," I sing.

Nolan's realization happens in slow motion, and it's a beautiful thing to witness. His eyes sparkling, his lips curving, a shocked puff of breath falling from his mouth.

Then a whispered *wow.*

He closes the distance between us, padding across the sapphire rug. His arms circle my waist. He lifts me up in a huge hug and spins me around once. When he stops, we still embrace, holding on so damn tight.

"I think we're almost there," he says, and there's such relief and desperation in his tone.

"I think so too," I say, my voice nearly breaking.

He squeezes harder, sighing happily against my neck, a fluttery breath ghosting over my skin. "I need this so much. I really need to get my shit together." It's like a confession, the kind of thing you'd only share with your closest friend. Something that shows your soft underbelly, all the things you want to change when you look in the mirror.

"You do have your act together," I reassure him.

"Barely." He's so hard on himself. He has been for some time. In a family of overachievers, Nolan sees himself as the odd man out. His brother's an NFL quarterback. His father started his own business, which paid for part of their college tuition. "I'm the guy scraping by as I couch surf. Last time I had my own place, I shared it with three roomies, and it sucked."

"But maybe not much longer," I say, choking up too.

"I want to get my own place. I want to pay off this . . ." He can hardly bring himself to say it.

I swallow around the knot in my own throat. "I know. Trust me, I know. Same, same."

The student loan.

At least, that's what I call it.

"Me too," I echo, my chest tight, tears pricking the back of my eyes. "But it's happening. You figured this out. You found Dot and Bette, and you made this happen. You do have your act together."

Nolan tugs me closer, his arms tighter still.

I dip my face against his neck. He smells like sleepy mornings, and like our sex hours ago, and a little like me and him. My head is spinning, and my heart is cracking open.

I need to let go. All these emotions are churning like a gathering storm of wishes and wants, smashing into things I can't have.

Dalliances in duos don't work. Sex can ruin a friendship, and it can sure tank a partnership. Especially if one person—*raises hand*—suffers from out-of-control feelings.

Last night was surely just sex to him. But I know myself—it could be more to me, and that's why we need to leave it at one and done. We'll stay the course and make sure this career high goes even higher.

I untangle my octopus arms from his neck, slide them off him, step back.

Smoothing my hands over my shirt, I try to blink

away the emotional moment and focus on the rest of this day, then the next, then the one after that.

"We need to get on the plane and get home to plan more episodes. Maybe we can hit it hard around Wine Country to mix it up? Do some fresh reviews, have lots of fresh content for our new viewers?"

"Love it." He scratches his head, then holds up a wait-a-minute finger, those flecks in his hazel eyes saying he has a plan. But first he walks around the bed to grab his glasses from the nightstand and puts them on. "I wish our flight didn't leave so soon. What if we had time to visit a bunch of places in Vegas and get content from a new city?"

"Maybe we can change to a later flight," I suggest. "Do four or five reviews. Stock up."

A city-wide smile lights his face. "Brilliance and beauty," he says.

"Hustle and charm," I say, then point to the bathroom. "Get ready."

Ten minutes later, he's out of the shower, wearing peacock boxers that make me smile and ache at the same time.

I can't enjoy his animal-print boxers. I look away, pack up, and check the room for anything left behind.

Then we go, finding our rental car in the parking lot and tossing our bags into the trunk. Neither of us has said a word about the sex we had last night.

I know we can't happen again. But his silence seems to say he doesn't consider that on the table. I know that last night can't happen again, but my heart is a little hurt that he doesn't say he would . . . if we could.

Instead, we're moving on with barely a word. Isn't that kind of what he's done since Inés broke his heart? Since she deceived him, he's protected that organ in his chest with flirt, with swagger, with playboy ways.

I won't judge him, though. It takes two to tango, and I definitely danced with him last night. We did the fuck-trot all night long.

What I can do is this—get us back to where we were. Where we need to be.

We crossed a line but that doesn't mean we can do it again. Sex leads to feelings and feelings lead to problems and problems lead to shows falling apart right as they're finding their audience.

There will be no more rocking the boat by rocking the bed.

Someone needs to say it. Before he turns the key in the ignition, I clear my throat. "About last night . . ."

His hazel eyes flash with vulnerability and a bit of longing. "Yeah?"

I swallow past a dry patch in my throat. "Well . . . you know." I wince. I can't bring myself to say *That was a mistake,* or *We can't do it again,* even if maybe he feels that way.

Perhaps he senses how hard this is for me. He jumps in, his tone a little heavy. "You were going to say it can't happen again?"

I sigh, both grateful and sad. "Way to read my mind."

"I didn't have to read your mind. I could read your face. It's all over your expression and in your eyes."

Even if he's not saying *I want you again but have to resist you,* I think it's in his eyes too. I can't be the only one who wants what I shouldn't—can't—have. "You're thinking it, too, aren't you? I mean, there's just so much—"

"—at stake," he supplies.

I nod, my throat tight again, my chest jittery. "Exactly." I gesture to the dashboard as if to indicate the world beyond our sex-capade. "Everything is happening for us at last."

"And we need to focus on that," he adds, more certain now.

I inhale sharply. "So that's what we'll do. The work."

"Yeah," he says, nodding. "The show means the world to both of us. Right?"

It sounds like he's begging me to agree, and I do. I want this show to take off for so many reasons. For my sister, for Nolan, for me.

"The show means the world," I echo. I can't let this chance slip away just because I'm into him.

I only wish I felt a little less achy as we change our flight, tackle the city, and check out as many cool, divey eateries as we can with the extra time.

Later that night, exhausted and energized, we board our Super Saver flight back to San Francisco. I buckle in. Nolan does the same. A peacock sits two rows behind us. I try not to laugh, but I crack up anyway.

Nolan nudges me, whispering, "Admit it. You're thinking of my boxers."

"Obviously."

"I guess you know my secret now," he says, his gaze drifting to his crotch as if his only secret is the style of briefs he wears.

He closes his eyes, and he feels miles away behind those glasses.

I want to know his other secrets too. Every now and then, I want to tell him the truth about my student loan, but I don't know if I could get the words out without sounding foolish.

Would he tell me his secrets if I told him mine?

Last night, I showed him some of mine. The things I want in bed. That I want to be hurt a little bit, to feel a little pain.

More than that, I showed him how much I want him.

But, as the plane soars into the inky night sky, I box up those wants and set them on a shelf.

10

WELL, THAT GOT AWKWARD FAST

Nolan

Emerson and I have been a lot of things to each other. When we met, she was the funny, bold, freckled brunette who lived in the freshman dorm next to mine. She knew all the lyrics to *Les Mis* and liked to eat Cinnamon Life Cereal for a late-night snack, but not the Lucky Charms I loved because the marshmallows in it are made with meat. Which was a gross thing to learn, but it didn't stop me from scarfing down the cereal.

Over the years, we've been pranksters, rearranging the furniture in Lauren and Dina's suite one night into the basement of the dorm.

We've been stress-meisters, freaking out over exams.

Since college, we've been wingmen and women, scoping out targets for each other in bars all over the city.

As life has ebbed and flowed, things with us have been fun, easy, happy and sad. Things have been quiet too, like when I was in France with Inés. Things have been just plain shitty, like when Emerson's twin sister died and my friend cried in my arms for weeks that spilled into months.

We've come in and out of each other's lives, but mostly in, and nearly always understanding each other.

Now, three days after Vegas, things are like this —*Really Fucking Awkward*.

As in, all caps. Six-story-billboard style.

Uncomfortable is the name of the game when she picks me up in Wanda outside Jason's house. The plan is to drive to Wine Country and visit a new diner.

"Hey," she says, a little distant.

"Hi," I say, a little laidback, hoping that'll help.

She pulls away from the curb in her tiny car, and the GPS chirps the directions.

"So, how's everything?" I ask, even though that sounds lame as fuck.

She arches a brow. "I saw you yesterday. The ice cream shop in Hayes Valley. Remember? Everything's still good."

"I know. I was just asking." Wow, that came out sounding defensive. "Can't I ask how you're doing?"

"Of course." She frowns as she heads toward the Golden Gate Bridge. "Sorry. I'm good. Great even. The views are insane. You?"

And we're all business.

Okayyy.

"Never better," I say, even though now it's the three

of us in the car—Emerson, me, and the strange tension between us.

So, this is how we do post-sex—awkwardly. Uncomfortably.

At the diner, we shoot our episode, testing a few dishes. She declares the quinoa bowl a *taste fiesta* in her mouth, and I have no immediate flirty retort for that.

What's wrong with me?

But the rest of the episode is solid, so hopefully no one will notice I am off my game.

I hit cut and end the recording, and Emerson and I turn our attention to the folks there to see us.

A line snakes out the door—plenty of guys and gals our age, lots of women in their early twenties. Some older fans too, more Dot and Bette's age, which is awesome. We've never really drawn that demographic before. I'd also say we have double the fans we drew before the promotion, maybe triple.

We take pics, chat, and sign shirts, and I say *fuck you* to the awkward because this life is better. I am starting to say goodbye to the cusp, and it feels good.

Until a cute blonde straggler at the end of the line reaches us. Her eyes drift from Emerson to me. "Are you free after this, Nolan? Or are you guys dating?"

Damn. Talk about direct.

Emerson gives a closed-mouth sliver of a smile. "He's just a friend," she says, patting my shoulder. Then she turns away and packs her bag.

"So, would you like to get a drink?" the woman asks, and I do admire her chutzpah. It's not easy to ask out a stranger, even if you think you know them from their online presence.

"Thanks, but I'm pretty busy with the show," I say.

The diner owner gives us some takeout as we leave, and we thank her. Emerson and I load our gear into the back seat of her tiny contraption of a car, tucking the food at my feet as I sit in the passenger seat, my legs folded up uncomfortably.

"Sorry for the . . . size of Wanda," she murmurs, something she usually says. Her car can feel like a thimble to me, but it does the job.

"You don't have to apologize for that," I say. "Just be glad we have wheels to get to Wine Country."

She doesn't answer while she busies herself weaving through afternoon traffic in the town square. "You know, if you ever want to say yes to someone, you can," she offers, a little strained.

I scoff. "What?"

She flaps her hand toward the diner. "Back there. I'm just saying."

"Yeah, I get it. And, um, same to you, I guess."

"Thanks?" she says, but it's a question.

"You're welcome?" I ask, and why the hell am I making that a question too.

Emerson turns onto a winding road that curves past vineyards. "I mean, that's what we decided, right?"

My chest tightens, irritation threading through me. "That's what we decided," I agree crisply.

"It's for the best," she says as if I need reminding.

"I know. Trust me, I know."

We're silent for one mile, then another, then several

more. That's awkward too. We aren't silent people, but now there's this heavy quiet hanging like a thick blanket between us. It's suffocating, and I reach to my collar like I can loosen a tie I'm not wearing.

There are a thousand things to talk about—the show, the traction it's getting, the thank-you pies Dot and Bette sent us, the emails from Hayes saying he's in various talks . . . There's our own wish to shoot again in New York someday. A year ago, we did a week of episodes there. Maybe we can find a sponsor for a few more Big Apple videos.

But I don't broach any of those topics. Instead, I stretch a hand to the Bluetooth speaker. "Want to listen to music?"

"Yes." The answer is immediate, like she's underscoring a potent wish to fill the silence with anything but our voices.

The car fills with the sound of The Wallflowers. Maybe that's an olive branch, that she picked a favorite band of mine rather than *Rent* or *Wicked*.

Maybe it's a sign that this awkwardness will pass. Please, let it pass soon.

A couple days later, we're at a new salad bar in Oakland, and as we shoot, I wax on about the chicken meat in the salad.

"You love your meat," she says, all sass and vitriol.

My eyes widen. That's gotta be good. A sign we're getting back on track.

I arch a brow and counter, "So do you."

I lay on the flirt before I consider the extra innuendo. For a second, Emerson's face goes pink, her expression morphing into something serious.

Shit. Is on-camera awkward going to be a regular thing now?

She's silent for a beat longer than I'd expect, then she squares her shoulders. "You think so?"

And she came to play ball. *Batter up*. "I sure do," I say.

"I suppose, but only certain kinds," she says in her trademark purr.

Wait. Is she talking about my dick? Well, the fucker seems to think so because he's sitting up in my jeans. Thank God for tables.

The fans shout their approval of our banter.

"Is Nolan giving you a foodgasm?" someone asks.

The pink in Emerson's cheeks races up the color palette to cherry.

But she rolls with it, giving a saucy flick of her hair. "Nolan always gives me foodgasms," she says, all slow and drawn out, and not helping along any deflation.

When we're done shooting, I take a minute to let the effect of her wear off, then we pose for photos as usual. At the end of the line is a bearded dude in cuffed-up jeans who saunters over to Emerson then points to me. "Hey, are you two a thing?"

I clench my fists. Why the hell is he asking?

"We're just friends," Emerson says with a cool grin.

Smirking, he lasers his focus solely on her. "Ah, so that means—"

"No. It means no," I cut in.

The guy holds up his hands and backs away. "Sorry, dude."

When he's gone, she gives me a *what gives* look. "Really, Nolan?"

"Oh, were you into him?"

She narrows her eyes. "That's not the point."

"What's the point then?"

"Don't talk that way to a fan," she whispers as she drops the tripod into her backpack.

"You say it to women all the time." That feels a little *I know you are but what am I* and I hate it.

"No, I say *we're just friends,* and I say it nicely."

But men should not be coming on to her. "Em, that dude was hitting on you, so I made it clear you're not available."

Backpack on, she crosses her arms. "Is that for you to decide?"

"So that's it? That's the issue?" I bite out, thoroughly frustrated with this conversation and my own role in it. "Did you want to go out with him?"

"No. But that's not the point."

"It kind of seems like it is," I say.

"The point is I'm a grown woman with a mouth of my own. A big mouth, thank you very much. I can answer for myself. I can turn him down myself. As you know, I can be a dick if I need to. But that wasn't a situation that called for one." With a huff, she points down the block. "I'm going to the coffee shop next door to edit."

"I'll do the socials," I mutter.

We settle at the same table in the café, where

Emerson drains her espresso in two sips then sets it down with a loud *thunk*. Silence wraps around her as she taps away on the screen. *Tap, tap, tap*.

She hammers the keys, punctuating the quiet.

But I have nothing to say because I'm picturing her dating that bearded guy with the rolled-up pants. Or some other dude. Some boring toad like her ex, John, or that dick she dated a year ago who fell for someone else while he was with her. Hayden, or Butthead, or Shit for Brains. I don't even want to remember his name.

I grind my teeth as I answer fan messages.

She huffs as she edits.

Then, she closes the laptop. "You know, you can see someone if you want," she says tightly, like the words don't quite fit on her tongue.

I take off my glasses and pinch the bridge of my nose. "Emerson. I'm not going to see anybody now. I haven't seen anybody in a while. All I give a shit about is the show and getting rid of this stupid fucking awkwardness between us, okay?"

Her lips are a ruler. "Me too."

I've said the wrong thing yet again. I think I know the right thing—it's been working through my brain for a few minutes now—but I have to say it. Since Emerson does have a big mouth, and she used it to make a point —one I ignored.

"I'm sorry," I tell her. "I shouldn't have said anything to that . . . *guy*." I grumble the last word. "It wasn't my place, and you're right. You have a huge mouth, and you're perfectly capable of turning a dickhead down."

Her expression softens, and her lips part. "Why do you assume he's a dickhead?"

"Because you have terrible taste in men," I say.

She rolls her eyes. "Tell me something I don't know."

I want to tell her, *You can't be with another guy who doesn't get you. Or respect you. Or treat you well.* Instead, I say, "So, I'll let you break their hearts next time."

"Gee, thanks."

My gaze stays locked on hers. "Let's just . . . get back to how we were, okay?"

She gives a faint smile, maybe one of relief. "I'm sorry too. Sorry that things have been weird." She swipes a hand across her cheek, then lets out a long breath. "It's just . . . I don't do casual sex, Nolan. I don't know how to act afterward."

It's a confession, and I'm damn grateful. Finally—fucking finally—we're talking about the elephant in the room.

"I get it," I say softly, reaching for her hand, squeezing it. In a friendly way. "Let's just be ourselves? We've done it for years. We can do it again."

"Yeah, I know. I'm sorry; this was stupid. I'm not interested in seeing anyone either." Then she laughs. It's a wonderful sound, a relieved sound, and her shoulders relax. "I think we needed to be really awkward and weird."

"Maybe we did," I say with a smile.

She grins too, her eyes lively. "I mean . . . the sex was great. But this friendship is better. Irreplaceable." She gestures from her to me. "Just being able to talk to you freely. Right? I don't want to lose it. That's what matters."

I park my hands behind my head, lasering in on one thing. "So, you thought the sex was great?"

She rolls her eyes and throws a napkin at me. "You're such a guy."

"I am."

Just like that, all the awkwardness leaves the premises.

Too bad I still want her. But you don't always get what you want.

* * *

That night, I grab a bus and head to the ballpark, clicking on my news app along the way to catch up on what I like to call *Stories That Don't Want to Make Me Stab My Eyes Out.*

I've carefully culled the articles served up to me to include developments in food science, the weirdest new eateries, uplifting animal stories, updates in green energy, and listicles I can't resist, like *Seven Breakfast Cereals You Have to Eat Before You Die* and *Twenty Best Autocorrects Ever*.

Hmm. Do I want to read about The Green Ant, a new pop-up restaurant in New York that serves organic insects, or an ode to why Cinnamon Toast Crunch is life-changing? As my thumb hovers over the BuzzFeed list, a text pops up from TJ.

I pick door number three: a text from a friend.

. . .

TJ: True fact—you were wondering if Emerson was thinking of your dick on your show today when she said *only certain kinds.*

Nolan: True fact—you are a warlock.

TJ: Yes! My mind-reading superpower is top-notch.

Nolan: Is that really what you want for a superpower? Mind-reading? A mind is usually a filthy place.

TJ: I'm all for mining filth. Makes my job easier. Inspiration, baby! Also, it kills you that I can tell what's going on in your pretty little head. So, the amusement factor works for me too.

Nolan: Awesome. I'm just a circus monkey to you.

TJ: Accurate. Also, I have this extra box of Count Chocula in my cupboard from the last time you were here. Want me to save it for you?

Nolan: Guess who can read minds now? That question means . . . wait for it . . . you miss me!

. . .

TJ: Not. At. All.

Nolan: Cool. I don't miss any of you assholes in New York either.

That is a huge lie. I do miss my buds in New York, and I had a blast when I was there solo a few months ago.

Wouldn't mind being back there now.

Sometimes New York feels like it's mine, a place where I could do what the song says—*make it there.*

Tonight, I just need to make it to the ballpark, so I shoot the breeze with TJ for a few more stops then bound off the bus when the stadium comes into view.

My dad's waiting outside the gates—he's taking Jason and me to a Cougars baseball game tonight. He grabs beers for us, then guides us to the seats he snagged at the first-base line.

Dad only sits in the best seats.

Drinks the best beer.

Has the best kids.

Jason points to the field. "I'll be with you guys in a minute. I need to say hi to Grant."

"Show-off," I tease.

My brother just shrugs and smiles as he makes his way to the edge of the stands to chat with the team's starting catcher, one pro-baller to another.

Once I sit, my dad parks a hand on my shoulder.

"Shall I call you King of the Home Page, son?"

It's a compliment of sorts, but I don't like talking work with him. "Sure, Dad. That won't be weird at all," I say drily.

"You're getting there. But you know my offer stands," he says, lifting his beer and taking a long pull.

This is why I don't like talking work—because he'll make me an offer once again.

"I know, and I appreciate it. But hey, do you think the Cougars will extend their winning streak tonight?" I ask.

I know what's next. The fatherly pat. The serious look. The worry in his eyes. I try to avoid it, but I can't.

"I mean it, son. Do you need any help? I've got franchises opening in Palo Alto, Menlo Park, Pier 39, Sausalito . . . You can take your pick of Mister Cookies."

My father built a cookie business from scratch years ago. The shop franchises put my brother and me through college. It funded our lives. He's the classic self-made man, doing it all, taking care of his kids.

"No, I'm fine. Things are taking off," I say, knocking back some more beer as I check out the animated race cars on the jumbotron. Jason is still chatting with the catcher.

"That's fantastic," my dad says. "It's amazing how quickly you guys have risen to the top." Unspoken, but there, is the implication that we could fall just as quickly, and that when we do, he'll be waiting.

A weight sinks in my gut. Cookies are awesome, but I don't want to run a cookie franchise. I don't want shit handed to me.

My brother didn't have anything handed to him.

My dad didn't either.

"Or you could just crash on Jason's couch forever," Dad says with a wink.

I tense as my little brother bounds up the aisle, taking the steps in twos.

"Did Jason say something to you? Like he doesn't want me there?" I ask Dad quietly.

But my brother has eagle eyes and ears. "Yeah, I said, 'Please get rid of my personal chef. It's so hard when he's there.'" Jason drops in the seat next to me and gives me a noogie. "Dude, you are welcome, like, forever."

Ah, fuck. I love this guy so damn much. Emerson is right. Jason has never once given me a hard time about his paying for cooking school and then my not being a chef.

And yet, I don't want to be his personal chef any more than I want to be a cookie man. I need to get my own place again. Something that's just mine. I need my own career—one I launched with hard work and no handouts.

I picture the latest letters from the bank for that dumbass IOU, the *due soon* notice stamped on the statements. Jason would pay it in a heartbeat, but I won't ask him.

Nope. No fucking way.

It's up to me. I have to pay off this last debt on my own, and I have to make this show with Emerson a success. There are no other options.

If I sleep with her again, I'll fuck up this chance.

11

DON'T YOU DARE CRY

Emerson

When my father crosses the finish line on his bike on Saturday morning, my mom cheers, her arms high in the air. "Woohoo, William!"

"Such a fangirl," I tease.

"Of course I am," she says.

Dad blows her a kiss, then stops, unclips his shoes, and gets off his road bike. Wheeling it beside him, he closes the distance and hugs her. He's sweaty and clearly tired from the race through Marin County to Sausalito, but still pumped.

"Raised five thousand dollars," he says, emotion in his voice.

"I'm proud of you, Dad," I say, smiling from deep within my soul.

He tugs at his shirt, emblazoned with the primary

charity behind the bike race—a hospital where Callie was treated for her heart condition. They took good care of her, especially at the end. They took care of me too, when they tested me for it. But Callie was the unlucky twin—the one with a congenital heart defect that ended her life at twenty-eight years. I was fit as a fiddle, able to ride roller coasters, run, swim, hike, and play.

Live.

"Be right back, sweetheart," he says to my mom, then heads to the race organizer's table to finish up paperwork.

We stand by Richardson Bay, the wind cutting across the dark blue water. "I talked to her the other night," my mom says offhand as she swipes some breeze-blown strands off her cheek.

My mom believes in angels, believes Callie is one. It's a nice idea, that someone is always around. Though I don't buy it, I don't dispel it either. "What did she say?"

"She had that twinkle in her eyes. A devilish grin. And she said, 'Are you impressed with what Emerson pulled off? Because I sure am.'"

My whole heart climbs up my throat. "Thanks, Mom," I whisper around the noose of emotions.

"Good job, honey. Your show is so cute. We're proud of you."

But would they be proud of me if they knew what I did before Callie died? How I spent the money?

Sometimes I think I make good decisions. And sometimes I make really dumb ones. Look at my track record with men. I've picked some serious duds.

Good thing I haven't quit my day job.

* * *

That afternoon, it's off to work I go. I add a few extra eyeshadow shades to my makeup bag and sling it on my shoulder. As I head for the door, my gaze drifts to my road trip photos. There's a shot of Callie and me in front of Rod's Steak house in Arizona, then a silly selfie of us leaving ten minutes later, laughing.

"Why did we come here? It's all meat," she'd said.

"I told you. I googled the menu," I said to her.

"It seems like there should be a veggie option."

"Yeah, this classic roadside diner screams black bean burger," I'd teased.

A faint smile tugs at my lips as memories of that trip flicker past me. "I'm glad you talk to Mom," I say to my empty apartment, then I leave for a wedding that should help me pay down the loan a little bit more.

An hour later, at a luxury hotel overlooking the ocean, I swipe the last slick of mascara on the bride, step back, and then spin her around to regard her face in the scalloped mirror. "Gorgeous, don't you agree?"

The pretty redhead nibbles on the corner of her lip and tries to suck in a tear.

Her maid of honor thrusts a tissue at her face. "Don't you dare cry, Angela," she says.

I smile at the two of them. "You don't want to ruin your wedding makeup," I say to Angela. "But don't worry. I'll stick around and touch you up for the photos after."

"Thanks. You did an amazing job," the bride says.

I'm grateful for that. Just in case the good run *How to Eat a Banana* is having turns out to be a sprint.

I wait in the hotel hallway during the ceremony, listening to a podcast, then a text pops up from my friend Jo in New York.

Jo: Stop me. I don't know if I can resist half-price tickets to the *Tommy* revival in three weeks.

Emerson: Don't resist. Get them. Get them now.

Jo: Enabler. Can you come? Please?

Emerson: I wish, but I don't know that I can get away.

Jo: Makeup gigs keeping you busy? Or food gigs?

Emerson: All of the above. I want to do New York again soon. And to see you. It's been too long.

Jo: I demand you come here sooner rather than later. But I get that you're busy. How is work, though? Things with Nolan seemed . . . less festive in that Wine Country diner episode. Not that I'm studying every single detail, but you two have just seemed . . . not quite as close lately? A bit tense.

Oh. Shit.

Emerson: Really?

Jo: Yeah. The last one was better with the salad, but still, I wanted to ask if you're doing okay?

That's a damn good question, but I flash back to yesterday at the coffee shop and the way we worked through the tension and finally talked it over. Yet if the friction was obvious on camera, that's confirmation that we can never get naked together again. I can't let the show be affected at all.

Emerson: We're all good. Just busy.

I close the text thread and turn off my phone. It's photo time for the newlyweds, and I need to focus on the job, not on the fact that I'm terrible at hiding my emotions. Stupid fucking emotions.

When the gig ends, I leave the hotel and turn my phone back on. A text blinks up at me.

Nolan: Where the hell are you? Our agent is calling in thirty minutes. Says it's big news. I'm at Jason's.

I race over like the wind.

12

I DON'T EVEN REALLY LIKE BANANAS

Emerson

At Jason's house, it's a Frisbee and barbecue evening for the host, so the backyard is brimming with pro-footballers and their significant others, if they have them. There are guys from Jason's team, the Hawks, and guys from the city's other team too, the Renegades.

Like Harlan, the just-retired star receiver who's married to my friend, Katie. His rookie replacement, Carter, is here with his girlfriend, Sydney.

Everyone's in the yard, goofing off as the sun dips lower in the sky, except for Nolan and me. We're inside, on pins and needles.

From my spot in the kitchen, I stare out the window, zooming in on Harlan as he easily slings a Frisbee to Jason, then on Katie, who works the grill like a pro, flipping burgers and chicken. She does everything well, so no surprise there.

I watch them and wait for our agent to pick up the phone.

I have to focus on something other than the Extremely High Levels of Impatience flooding my veins as we dial Hayes again.

The connection went dead a minute ago in the middle of our call, right as he was laying out, oh, you know, life-changing details. As it rings and rings, I jerk my gaze away from the glass and meet Nolan's eyes. Bright, wide, hopeful.

Like a mirror.

"This can't really be happening," I say, and I'm not sure I'm even in my body. It's like I'm floating above us in a fevered, crazy dream. One I don't want to wake from because it's just so damn good here in this altered state.

I hope it lasts.

I really do.

"I think it's finally happening, Em," he says, kind of hushed and wonderstruck.

Another ring.

Then, Hayes's voice crackles over the speakerphone. "Hey, hey! I hit a dead spot in my building," our agent says, tinny at first, then he smooths out. "So, what do you think? The terms are good. The opportunity is huge. And they want you to start right away."

Nolan's grin is electric. "It's sort of a no-brainer, isn't it?"

"Well, I wouldn't say a zombie could do this deal, but . . ." Hayes chuckles.

"I don't think he meant it like that," I chime in, laughing too, maybe even slap-happy.

Is this real?

Is our agent talking terms of a streaming deal with us?

I pinch my arm to make sure I'm alive. That this call is occurring on Planet Earth and not in Emerson's Fantasy Parallel Universe.

"Yeah, we definitely need your non-zombie brain, Hayes," Nolan says.

"Good. I advise you to say yes. This is everything we've been wanting for you two," he says.

It *is* everything.

That's what scares me. If something is too good to be true, maybe it is. But I set aside philosophical musings as Hayes reviews more details.

He gives us the details for our shoot and the meeting in New York with the Webflix producer, then he ends the call. As we hang up the phone, the sounds from the yard drift in. Jason's voice, Harlan's voice, Katie's, Carter's, Sydney's.

But the one voice I key in on belongs to the person in front of me.

My best friend.

"Emerson," Nolan rasps, and my name has never sounded so charged, so full of atoms and ions.

Full of hopes and dreams.

He advances toward me. Clasps my shoulders. "Did

we just get an offer from Webflix to do our very own streaming show in New York City?" he asks in disbelief.

He sounds so fucking giddy.

He sounds how I feel.

"I think we did," I whisper, like saying it too loud will tank the deal. Like it's a precious thing we have to whisper about to protect.

"This must be what it feels like to be my brother and play in the NFL. To be my dad and close killer deals," he says.

I grab his face, hold him tight. "Shut up. Don't compare yourself. This is what it feels like to be *us*."

"I like *us*."

I do too. I like the feel of his face in my cupped palms. I like his hazel eyes, glittering. I like sharing this passion project with him.

I'm so glad I'm not doing this solo. I was never wired to be alone. I traveled into this world as part of a team. I'm built to be part of a duo.

And we did this together.

"So do I," I say, as a marching parade takes over my heart. Drums beat, trumpets flare, and I am exuberant. "I feel like I did that night after you took me on the roller coaster."

Is that too risky to say? Maybe it is. But I feel a little high right now. A little daring, like I can have it all.

"Me too." He steps closer. It's a declaration as he invades my space, inches away. Kisses are written all over his eyes, as if this is how we need to seal the deal. Like we did after the roller coaster. Hell, we survived our first kiss; we survived sex. We could surely handle a celebratory kiss.

I'm ready to throw caution to the wind, right here in his brother's kitchen. My stomach flips, and my chest flops, and both Nancy and I are in agreement.

With his face still in my hands, I lean into him, a gust of breath coasting over my lips. It sounds like an admission. Like my sigh says *kiss me.*

Lord knows, my body says it as I tilt my face and wait.

Wait. Wait.

It's that heady moment when two people edge together. When you watch a movie or a show, and the inevitable, slow, intoxicating slide into a kiss begins.

He's so close I can smell his aftershave. My mouth aches for him.

And I want to get lost in a kiss.

"Who needs some more of the world's finest potato salad?" Harlan's voice slices through the air as the back door swings open.

We wrench apart.

"Hey, now. I've been eyeing that cherry pie you brought. You better not hold out on me," Jason chimes in.

That's all it takes.

We move away from each other like we've been scalded. Frustration takes over for a beat, but then that excited energy returns because *holy shit. We just got ourselves a deal.*

The guys stroll into the house, shoes slapping as they near the kitchen, followed by Katie and Sydney.

"Oh, you're finally going to let yourself put cherries in that temple of a body," Harlan teases Jason.

Jason gestures to his big frame. "I've been known to corrupt this temple from time to time," he says.

Harlan hoots then points dramatically to the counter. "Let the corruption begin. Get this man a slice of the best cherry pie ever," he says, grabbing the pink box with one of his famous homemade pies inside.

The former star player bakes with his young daughter in his spare time, and from what Katie tells me, that's an ovary-melting sight. No wonder Katie's preggers.

"Oh, hey there," Harlan says on the path to the pie, maybe noticing us for the first time. He stops in his tracks, shooting me a *what's up?* look. "Did we interrupt something devilishly important? From the looks of it, you two were making predictions for the next football season or debating whether dark chocolate is better than milk."

"Dark chocolate," Nolan says quickly.

Jason looks from Nolan to me, his eyes a clock pendulum as he assesses us shrewdly, like he assesses plays on the field. "Wrong answer. Milk chocolate," he teases, then the guys beeline for the pie, bypassing the potato salad.

Katie's the only one who seems to understand the intensity of this moment. "What's going on? You look like you've just won an Oscar," she says, tilting her head.

"I feel that way," I blurt out. Then I let the good news —*great* news—rush through my body one more time, and I stand a little taller. "You're looking at the stars of the next new restaurant show on the world's biggest streaming service. Webflix just picked up our show for a season, and they want us to film it in New York for a month."

Katie screams in excitement. "Yes! I knew it, friend! I knew it!"

Harlan high-fives me. "Congratulations, you badass people."

Jason strides across the kitchen to wrap his big brother in a hug. "Dude! So proud of you."

My heart climbs up my throat as I watch the two of them share the joy.

Just look at this. Look at what we have. And I nearly threw it all away for a kiss.

We crack open beers and wine, and Katie grabs a soda, then we move to the living room, where there is pie and laughter and excitement.

Jason lifts his beer, toasts to us, then to Nolan. "To the guy who's always had my back since I was fourteen. You know what I'm talking about. You know it. And I fucking love you, and I fucking knew you'd get here," he says, voice thick with emotion as he clinks glasses with Nolan. "That's why I bet on you."

"You did, man. And of course I had your back," Nolan says quietly. He dips his head, a little embarrassed, but there's such sweetness, such brotherly love between them. I'm pretty sure I know what Jason must be talking about at age fourteen, but now's not the time to ask Nolan or Jason for details, so I file those comments away.

Jason clears his throat, then rubs his palms together.

"Who wants more pie and a viewing sesh of the best of *How to Eat a Banana?*"

Katie waves a hand high. "I do! I do! Can we play along and guess what the hosts will rate the food?"

"Hell, yes," Carter says.

"I'm in," Sydney adds.

Jason grabs the remote, flicks on the big screen, and toggles over to YouTube.

"Home page champions . . . of the world," he sings, channeling Queen for a moment.

Jason plays some of our funniest episodes, and our friends make a drinking game of guessing our ratings. Then YouTube auto-plays into an older episode, before Nolan's time.

One of Callie and me demonstrating the fine art of eating a banana.

For a second, I freeze, expecting it to hurt to watch my sister and me as we peel back the skins on our respective fruit.

"There is no way to be classy as you eat this," Callie says.

On the screen, I laugh. "Babes, no one ever said eating a dick-shaped fruit was classy."

And in Jason's living room, I breathe out.

It doesn't hurt.

I don't ache at seeing us.

I feel just fine.

Hell, I feel good.

No one goes quiet. No one says *rest in peace*. Instead, Harlan points at the screen, laughs, then nudges his wife. "Darling, I'd like to watch you eat a banana," he stage-whispers.

"You're so romantic," she tosses back.

Jason stretches an arm across the back of the couch. "I like bananas," he says with a cheeky grin.

Nolan smacks his shoulder. "Dude, I've known that since you were fourteen."

That earns Nolan a noogie, as it should.

I smile, letting some of the anxiety I've felt lately fade and the worry and the what-ifs tiptoe away.

* * *

Later, when it's just Nolan and me in the kitchen cleaning up, he says, "Thanks for letting me do the show with you."

I roll my eyes because sometimes it's easier than being serious. "Please. Thank you for being my banana," I tease. "You're my main banana." I pause as I wipe down the counter. "Deep thoughts. Is it weird that I don't even really like bananas?"

His expression goes intensely serious. "More proof we were meant to do this show together. I, too, believe bananas are overrated as fruit."

"How did I not know you felt this way?"

His eyes twinkle. "Apparently, there are things you still have to discover about me. But allow me to help. The top of the fruit scale starts at peaches, cherries, and strawberries."

"And blueberries and blackberries are right there too."

"Exactly. And bananas are down low," he says, pushing his hand toward the floor to demonstrate.

"Don't be knocking bananas," Jason calls out from the living room.

"We know, we know," Nolan shouts back.

That.

That makes me happy in a warm, fuzzy way. I'm not jealous he has this closeness with his brother when my sister's gone. I'm glad. So damn glad.

I love, too, that we have this chance. It's what Nolan needs to feel worthy.

I know he is. I just want him to know it for himself.

* * *

When I leave at the end of the night, Katie catches up to me on Jackson Street and pulls me aside under a streetlamp.

"So, I got the feeling we interrupted something when we came in from the yard," she says, her eyes wide and inquisitive.

I gulp in a breath of night air. "Yeah, here's the thing . . ."

She arches a brow. "Oh. There's a thing?"

No point lying. I don't want to hide the truth from my friend. "We slept together in Vegas."

Her big eyes go bigger. "And how would you rate the sex on your food scale?"

A wonderful, warm sensation zips through me. The memory of Nolan climbing on top of me, going deep in me, fucking me, taking me. "Seismic. It was seismic."

She shimmies her hips. "Well, that complicates things," she deadpans.

"It did, but we're fine now. We agreed it won't happen again. So, I'm trying to put the genie back in the bottle," I say.

She takes a beat to study my face, looking for whether I believe what I just said, perhaps. "And does the genie fit?"

"Sometimes. Other times, the genie is sticking its legs out and its hands, and it's kind of flailing around," I say, a little helpless, a lot honest.

"It's hard stuffing genies back in bottles," she says, speaking the truth.

It's hell. But it has to be done. "But necessary."

"I know, sweetie. I know." She pulls me in for a hug. "Good luck."

She gives no great parting words of wisdom because some things in life are just hard. Like pretending you don't have massive feelings for someone.

I go home that night and pay some bills. This is what I'm supposed to be doing—carving out a life, a job, a career.

A future.

* * *

A week later, my bags are packed, and I say goodbye temporarily to this place I used to share with my sister.

There's a small photo book from our Route 66 road trip in my backpack and a ladybug charm hanging on my neck for luck.

Finally, I've got some luck, so I make a promise not to squander it.

I make that promise to myself.

* * *

When we land in New York, a handler named James meets us at the airport, escorts us into Manhattan, and helps us check into the hotel Webflix arranged for us.

We're staying on the twelfth floor, a couple of doors away from each other. Nolan and I step off the elevator, and I gesture to the right. "Confession: I did wonder if the network was going to put us in the same room. And how we would handle it. But hey, we have separate rooms after all," I say, giving him my best cheery grin when I turn to 1208, and he moves toward 1205.

No chance of an adjoining door. Damn shame.

I mean, damn good thing.

"Too bad. I was hoping we could face mask together," Nolan says, snapping his fingers, aw-shucks style.

It's a joke, but when he rearranges his expression a second later, he must realize, like I do, that face masks turned out to be foreplay.

His smile disappears.

Mine does too as a fresh burst of want blooms low in my belly.

Yes, good thing we have separate rooms. I steer the conversation to safer shores. "Meet you in the lobby in an hour? So we can head over to Gin Joint?"

"Yes," he says, and I shut my door.

My room smells fresh and clean, like jasmine and lemongrass.

No embalming clinics here.

Just a big king-size bed all to myself. It's quiet and mine, all mine.

A little later, I make my way to the lobby to meet Nolan. When I get off the elevator, I do a double take.

Dot and Bette are here too.

In the same hotel, with the same network handler who escorted us over earlier today.

13

THERE IS NO JUST

Nolan

"Get your butt over here right now, Nolan McKay!"

Not that I planned on ignoring Bette, but there's no one on earth who could deny her a hug right now.

Her arms stretch out wide; her smile wraps around the city. She's decked out in jeans and a San Francisco Hawks jersey with a pink gingham bandana pinning back her dark hair.

I cross the distance in the lobby, and she sweeps me up in a hug. "What the heck are you doing here, you cuties?"

Funny, I could ask the same of her and Dot.

And I'm dying to know.

The platinum blonde turns to me, parks her hands on her hips. "Exactly! To what do we owe the pleasure of seeing you sweeties again?" Her blue eyes swing around the lobby, landing on Emerson, right beside me.

There are more hugs, then James darts aside with a quick *excuse me* as he whips his phone from his pocket. Guess he won't be giving any answers.

"Webflix picked up our show," Emerson says brightly.

Dot's jaw drops.

Bette claps. "That is so fantastic. I'm so stinking happy for you. We got a show too. Can you believe it? Maybe we'll all be TV stars," Bette says, adding jazz hands.

A throat clears. "Dot. It's getting late. You need to get to sleep soon." It's the boss. Evelyn's telling it like it is, ordering her grandma and her grandma's friend around. The girl in fishnets and motorcycle boots seemed to just appear out of thin air. Maybe she's magic. I wouldn't be surprised.

"Sleep, yes, but what I also need is a nightcap. On the rocks. And a cup of cocoa for you, Ev," Dot says.

The teen rolls her eyes. Because of course she rolls her eyes.

"And the first photoshoot is at ten in the morning," Evelyn continues, then nods at me, then Emerson. "Good to see you two again."

"And you. But . . ." My brow narrows, and I try to figure out how Evelyn's pulling this off. "Don't you have school?"

She stares at me, her eyes saying *duh*. "Zoom. Obvs."

"Right. Obvs," I echo.

Evelyn ushers Dot and Bette away, and Emerson and

I leave the midtown hotel in a flurry, furtively glancing behind us as we push through the revolving doors.

Once we're out on the street, Emerson tugs my elbow, yanks me farther away, her finger on her lips.

"I don't think they can hear us now," I say out of the side of my mouth.

"You never know," she says, then when we're around the corner, she stops, flaps an arm in the direction of the skyscraper hotel. "What's going on? Something is up."

She sounds wildly suspicious, and maybe I should be too, but I want us to focus on our show, not on nefarious subplots we'll never untangle. "Looks like they got picked up too. I'm guessing Webflix is on a buying binge for food shows?" I suggest. That makes as much sense as anything. "We just have to do what we came here to do."

With her jaw set hard, Emerson seems determined to get to the bottom of it. "But both of us? At the same time? And we were together with them on YouTube." She lifts a skeptical brow. "It feels like something is going on."

I wouldn't bet against her, but I don't know who's bluffing and who's not. "Look, we don't know. But we're in New York again, and we have a meeting with the executive tomorrow. For tonight, let's see the crew."

That was my idea. Did I also arrange to get together with friends on our first night here for a particular reason?

Yes. Yes, I did.

The way I see it is the more time I spend with Emerson in a group, with cameras, with everyone around us, the less tempted I'll be to get her alone, back her against the door of 1208, dip my face to the soft skin of her neck, and tease her with my tongue and mouth.

Like I wanted to do in my brother's house a week ago.

Like I want to do now as we walk across Twenty-Third Street. Good thing walking and kissing is, well, not a thing.

Maybe I can just spend the next month walking, and I'll be able to resist kissing the breath out of her.

* * *

It's like a reunion at Gin Joint when TJ joins us along with Jo, Emerson's good friend. Easton and Bellamy are on their way, Jo notes as we grab a velvet couch and a man with golden pipes croons old standards on a piano.

As the guy in the dapper suit sings "Baby Won't You Please Come Home," Emerson wastes no time going full Agatha Christie. After we order drinks, she catches Jo and TJ up on the Dot and Bette sighting.

"So, what do you think? Why are they here?" Emerson asks our friends.

I laugh, pointing my thumb at her. "She can't ever stop working."

"But it's weird, right?" she asks, undeterred. "Feels like it has to be something."

TJ lifts his old-fashioned and swirls it, his brown eyes intense as he answers. "My advice? Don't try to figure out Webflix's intentions. You'll be wrong. Big companies like that have their own agendas, and you can't ever truly get to the core of them."

"Seriously," Emerson presses, rubbing her hands along her thighs, a sign she's getting worked up, "you're all about motivation. What do you make of Dot and Bette being here while we're here?"

"Emerson," I cut in, setting a hand on hers to try to calm her anxiety. "You're going to drive yourself nuts trying to figure this out."

Jo's blue eyes light up like sparklers. "Ohh! What if there's a new reality show? YouTube stars vie against each other on streaming services," she suggests.

"Not helpful, Jo," I mutter.

Emerson runs with it. "Right? Or what if Webflix is going to surprise us. *Hey, you're doing the show together!*"

"I highly doubt that," I say, reaching for my beer. "They would have told Hayes. So why don't we just ask him tomorrow when we see him for our intro meeting with Webflix?"

"Fine," Emerson says with a sigh that says she'll *only* let this go for now, not forever. "But I think it's something."

TJ lifts his glass in her direction. "You're right, though, Em. A cigar is never just a cigar. The powers that be at Webflix want something. They're putting pieces in motion to get what they want. Don't mistake it for anything else. We all do what we do because we want things. No one is ever motivation-less."

Someone's got to put a pin in this detective game, so I try once more. "C'mon, man. You don't think they're doing it because they just like both shows?"

TJ scoffs. "There is no *just.* We don't *just* avoid relationships. We don't *just* have issues with commitments. There's always a wound, always a reason, and always a motivation. And there's definitely no *just because.*"

Trouble is, he's probably right.

We are wired for fear. We are wired to avoid pain. We are wired to fuck up, and most of all, we are programmed to want.

Voraciously.

What I want is this.

Literally *this.*

New York, friends—and a chance.

* * *

The next morning, Emerson and I meet with the network executive overseeing our show at a smoothie shop on Madison Avenue.

"I feel like I should be in LA," Emerson whispers as we arrive at *Just Juice* on Madison Avenue to see Ilene Brancuso.

Snickering, I point to the sign. "Better tell TJ there is a just when it comes to juice."

Shoes click on the sidewalk, and I turn to Hayes, looking sharp in a purple shirt and black pants as he strides toward us.

He greets us, then motions us closer. "Listen, I've made some calls about the gingham grannies. No one is sharing any details with me yet, but I'll see what I can sniff out later today. For now, let's just go in there, tell her your ideas, and get sign-off. That's what matters."

"Of course," I say.

Emerson smiles. "I promise I won't be a dick."

Hayes claps her shoulder. "I'll hold you to it."

Inside the shop, a woman with pink hair and buff arms waves us over to her table. A large silver tumbler sits in front of her, a metal straw in it. "You must be our new stars," she says, then stands and shakes hands with all of us. "I'm Ilene." She gestures to her silver straw. "I bring extras. Straws are so gauche. But I have metal ones for everyone."

"That's great," Emerson says. "Straws are the devil. But they are fun for innuendo."

Ilene winks. "That's what we love about you. That naughty mouth of yours."

"And I'm not afraid to use it," she says.

"What can I get you two?" Ilene asks.

I squint at the minimalist menu behind the counter. Hard to pick between celery juice, kale juice, and clear juice, but I'm going to find a way to do it. "I had a coffee at the hotel. I'm good."

"Same here," Hayes says.

Ilene flicks her gaze to Emerson, her last hope. "You should try the clear juice," Ilene tells Emerson.

Emerson smiles thinly, then shrugs. "Sure."

A minute later, Ilene plonks a tumbler on the table, hands Emerson a metal straw, and says, "*Bon appétit*."

Emerson lifts the tumbler, takes a sip.

Ilene nods enthusiastically. "Really good, right?"

"Just yum," Emerson says, overly enthused.

Ilene takes another long drink of her just juice. "So, we want you to get cracking with our crew.

What have you got, what have you got, what have you got?"

Whoa. Did she just ask three times? She must really want to know. Good thing we came prepared. "I can send over a list of our top choices, but let me go through them now," I say, then rattle off our picks. "It's a mix of new restaurants, as well as those that are weird, off-the-beaten path, and a little bit sexy. We also wanted to feature the chefs at each place and tease out their stories."

"We've researched places where the chefs or owners are real characters, so we want to add that interview element, but keep it tongue-in-cheek," Emerson puts in.

"Since that's our style," I add.

"And we love your style!" Ilene shouts. Literally shouts. Then, the pink-haired turbo executive draws a big gulp of her beverage, nodding the whole time. "Perf. Your ideas are just perf." She finishes her juice, claps her hands, and whistles. "The chefs, the stories, the food judging. Gah, I just love it all. And the two of you." She shimmies her shoulders. "Your cha-cha-cha is just delish."

Actually, I don't think that's just juice. I think it's just coke.

"And I love all these big plans. Especially the *sex-ay* ones," Ilene adds, then leans into a long, dramatic pause. "Which brings me to my quest-tee-ohn-ay. I have to know. Are you two together?" She slaps up a hand in the air as a stop sign. "Wait. I can't ask that. I'm not allowed. Don't answer." She covers her ears. "Tra la la."

Emerson and I trade *what-the-hell-is-happening*

glances.

Hayes mouths *she's excitable.*

No shit.

When Ilene removes her earmuffs, she folds her hands, takes a deep breath. "Just keep that magic *je ne sais quoi* between you two going. Know what I mean?" She adds an exaggerated wink.

The cha-cha-cha made it quite clear to me what she means, so I simply nod.

Emerson hums like she's taking this all in. "Yeah, I think I do."

When the meeting ends, Ilene blows air kisses, then darts out.

"She wants us to be Rachel and Ross," Emerson says in her wake. "She wants that sexy sitcom/are-they-or-aren't-they energy. Right?"

Hayes cuts in. "No one is saying you need to change things up. Just be yourselves. And if being yourselves involves flirting like you've always done, so be it."

"But what she's saying is sex sells. Right?" Emerson presses. She hasn't yet met a question she's afraid to ask.

He shakes his head, wags a finger. "No. What sells *more* is not knowing if the couple is sleeping together. What sells is mystery. What sells is the what-if. And on that note, I have another meeting."

He leaves, and I meet Emerson's green eyes, seeing all sorts of what-ifs, and knowing, too, that I can't have them.

I swallow them down, gesture to her silver tumbler. "How was it?"

She shoves my shoulder. "You sneak."

"Ouch!" I pretend it hurt.

"Why did you make me fall on that *Just Juice* sword?"

Ah hell. I can't resist. "You love swords."

That earns me a well-deserved eye roll. *"I had coffee,"* she says, imitating me.

"Well, why didn't you try to get out of it like I did?"

"I was trying to be nice to, oh, you know, the executive in charge of our show."

"Aww. Was that hard for you? Being nice?" I tease.

She shoves my other shoulder. "Almost impossible."

I adopt an intensely serious expression. "I'm so proud of you. Your devotion to the cause is truly admirable," I say. "The cause of *How to Eat a Banana."*

"And now the cause is us sorta, maybe acting . . . *sex-ay?"* she asks, imitating Ilene.

"Yeah. I mean," I say, lifting a hand to brush a chestnut strand from her shoulder, "it shouldn't be hard, should it?"

She bites her bottom lip, shakes her head. "It shouldn't be. That's the problem."

Yeah, it is the problem, so I change the subject. "So, what was in that juice?"

"Water, Nolan. Just water."

* * *

The next morning, I wake early to go for a run. In the lobby, I do a double take when I spot a familiar bearded, bespectacled guy trundling a suitcase across the marble floor to the elevator banks.

The Wine Dude. Marcos Ramirez is one of the

YouTube stars I considered reaching out to about the contest.

"Marcos," I call out, and he turns to me.

"Hey, man. You're in New York again?" he asks after we bump fists.

"I am. Just doing a thing for Webflix."

His dark eyes light up behind his glasses. "For real? Same here."

Good thing Emerson isn't here. Her Spidey senses would tingle and then erupt. "That's awesome. You've got a show with them?"

He crosses his fingers. "Here's hoping it pans out, but it looks that way. I paired up with Drive-Thru Babe on that YouTube contest, and well, long story short—"

"—she's here too?"

"You'll probably see her any day now," he says.

"Are you two doing a show together?"

"No, but supposedly I need to add all sorts of how-to wine stuff to my show. How to buy wine, how to pick wine, how to pair it with sandwiches. Beyond the quickie reviews I did on my channel."

And the plot thickens. "Good luck, man," I say.

"Let's grab a drink while you're here," he says.

"As long as it's not a red, a white, or a rosé," I agree with a wink.

"You wine hater," he calls out.

"You know it," I say, and as I run through Central Park, I text Hayes, asking him to get some details.

Pretty please and stat.

He writes back in seconds. *I'm on it; I've got calls out. Will know more soon.*

I hope he calls back before Emerson runs into Drive-Thru Babe or anyone else. I don't want her freaking out before we know the score.

Once I finish my run and shower, I gather her up and get her out of the hotel and away from any more potential random run-ins.

We spend the morning holed up in Doctor Insomnia's Tea and Coffee Emporium working on our first script, and I do my best to put YouTube star sightings out of my mind.

I manage it until Hayes calls me on FaceTime. I answer, grab my bag and step outside.

"Listen, I got the details on Dot and Bette and the others," he says.

Emerson joins me on the sidewalk, photobombing the call by sticking her face in front of my screen. "Tell us everything."

He's all serious as he answers. "Webflix is trying out a bunch of foodies from the YouTube contest. They'll run episodes of several shows, and whichever one is more popular . . ."

With a weary sigh, I finish the thought. "That's the one they'll pick up."

He nods. "Seems that way. Each one has a slightly different vibe. You're more food and flirt, but they also like the Dot and Bette grandma brand, and they're playing with new concepts for them too. Then there's the Wine Dude and the Drive-Thru Babe. There's also some guy named Max Vespertine. He's one of those Bourdain types. Rose up on Instagram, I guess. You know him?"

"No, never heard of him. But I'm jealous of his name," I say.

"Maybe I need to change my last name," Emerson offers, game for anything. "I mean, I can Google super-cool last names too. I could become Emerson Bardot. Emerson Raven. Or just Emerson X. Just off the top of my head."

Hayes smiles at her. "Emerson Alva is great. Don't change a thing. Just be yourself. You guys have come this far with a great concept, great energy, and great chemistry. Just keep it up."

"We will," I say, though it feels a little ironic that our partnership with Dot and Bette has now morphed into an *Amazing Race* competition. But there's no other way to see it. "It's a battle royale."

"Sometimes you have to fight for your seat at the table," Hayes says.

I'll have to look for my opening to do just that.

* * *

There's a new rhythm to the show in New York. We have a camera crew this time. We write out scripts. The crew spends more time shooting B-roll of restaurants, of the city, of us.

The show expands too. The segments are more in depth. We prep to do interviews with the chefs.

"What if we're not as good at the chef interview as Max Vespertine?" Emerson worries as we head down to Chelsea a week later.

"You think just because he has some uber-cool name that he's going to be as good as Bourdain?"

"It *is* kind of a hot name, and I watched all his videos. He's good. All broody thoughtful and intelligent," she says as we head onto the subway.

And hot? Is he hot too?

But if I ask that, I might as well wear a mood ring that turns green for jealousy. Instead, I nudge her and needle, "Aww, got a crush on him?"

She rolls her eyes. "Please. Those smarty-pants serious guys are not my type."

I can't help myself. "What's your type, then?"

She gives me the side-eye. "I believe you know."

"Do I?" Ah, hell. I hope she says *me*. I shouldn't want that, but I do.

"You said I had terrible taste in men. So obviously, my type is terrible men," she says, then gives me a sassy smile I want to kiss off her.

"Touché," I say.

As we get off at Fourteenth Street, she bats her lashes and licks her lips, playing it up. "But I suppose some might say you're terrible too, Nolan."

I laugh at her over-the-top flirting. "Keep that up for the cameras, Emerson Alva."

"I absolutely will."

If Ilene wants us to lean into the flirtation, she'll sure get it at today's stop—a restaurant that leaves little to the imagination.

Maybe this is our first opportunity to step up our game and throw down for that spot at the table.

Long Food restaurant, I'm ready.

14

LONG FOOD AND CHILDHOOD DREAMS

Emerson

Long Food in Chelsea, with the rainbow flag in the window, boasts a menu of phallic food. Popsicles, pickles, corn dogs, breadsticks, fried asparagus, and ice cream cones. It's so niche it's beyond niche.

But the pop-up restaurant is killing it with its marketing. The imagery all over Instagram of red lips and food like dicks lures the crowds.

A busty woman named Lucía runs the joint. She wears a black corset, her ample breasts spilling out over the top. Two men in matching leather vests prep the food while Lucía plucks a cherry-red popsicle from a freezer and presents it to us as an offering.

"Oh, baby. That better have my name written all over it," I say, making grabby hands.

"What if I want one too?" Nolan asks in his most charming voice.

"Bring this man a popsicle," I say as I take the red one, and the owner hands Nolan an icy treat as well.

"Yum."

I turn to my co-host. "But do you know what makes popsicles truly sexy, Nolan?" My eyes linger on his mouth while the camera captures our *je ne sais quoi.*

"Please share," Nolan says, encouraging me.

"It's not the licking or the sucking." I beckon him closer, playing it up for the audience too.

He leans in as called for in the script. "Tell me what makes them sexy."

I drag a finger along my bottom lip. "How it makes your mouth . . . so deliciously red."

Nolan doesn't answer right away—just stares at my lips, then blinks. "Like you've been kissed," he says.

"Hard and passionately," I add.

"Best kind of kissing," he says. The husky sound makes flames dance down my spine.

I don't know if we're saying our lines or living them.

I half wish I weren't attracted to Nolan. Mostly though, I wish I was alone with him. But I'm not, so all I can do is play it up for the camera. I lick the popsicle some more then give my killer groan.

"Mmm," I murmur. "So good."

My co-host stares hotly at me as I make out with the cherry ice, then he releases a long, heavy sigh laced with sexual frustration. Is that real or for the cameras?

"Yeah, I'd say that's pretty good," he says, his voice cracking.

It sounds as real as I feel, and I better judge this popsicle soon, or I'll need to stick it in my pants to cool off.

"I declare this an eight point seven five," I say, holding it high.

Nolan gives it a seven. "But would you do it again?" he asks.

Yes.

The thought of doing him again is too delicious to deny.

"Perhaps," I reply. "I could put this popsicle in my mouth over and over."

Because we have to give the network what they want.

Once we're done with the rating, we segue to the interview. Surely, talking to Lucía will be easier for Nancy and me to handle.

"So, why Long Food? What inspired you?" I ask.

The bosomy babe has confidence for days. She drags a bright pink nail along the counter, then her eyes drift to the two men in the vests cooking up corn dogs and prepping pickles. Her expression goes a little loopy and warm. "My two guys. We're together—the three of us. We like to have fun in all sorts of ways. I wanted people to come here and have a good time, and to think about maybe what they could do afterward," she says, owning her sexuality and her business, just like that.

I file that away—how she blends both those things, along with romance. This is a woman who is making it all work.

"So, food is foreplay," Nolan chimes in.

Lucía's warm brown eyes glitter. "It is if you let it be. Speaking of, you should try the strawberry shish kebabs dipped in chocolate," she urges with a purr.

Nolan turns his dreamy hazel gaze on me. "Want some?"

My chest feels all kinds of flippy from the question. Want *some*? I want *everything*.

"I do," I answer. If the viewers like "what-if," we'll give it to them.

The *what-if.*

Lucía hands him the chocolate-dipped stick of fruit, and he offers it to me. I bite into a juicy strawberry, savoring the taste of the chocolate and the fruit. A gust of breath coasts over his lips as I eat. If he were a cartoon hero, he'd be drooling puddles right now—a bespectacled, muscled, charming, hot nerd hero, his carved jaw all agape.

And . . . I'm fantasizing about cartoon men now.

Great. Just great.

Maybe that's part of the mystery for the audience—what happens with us after the cameras stop rolling—but that's a mystery to me too.

Possibilities crowd my brain. What if we didn't work together? What if I wasn't terrified of losing someone I love? What if I didn't want our show to succeed more than I wanted to get close to him again?

Now, there's a question—is the show what's holding us together or keeping us apart?

When Nolan peels away to chat with fans, I seize the chance to quiz Lucía about something other than food.

I'm a planner, after all, and I like to do my research. "Is it hard? Working together with your men?"

She scoff-laughs. "So hard. We don't always get along, honey."

"And what then?" I'm dying to know.

"We try to work through the problems."

"But the business . . . mixing it all," I press. "Do you worry?"

She gives a soft smile. "Only every day," she says, then pats my hand, squeezes it, and whispers, "Good luck."

I file that away too—it takes some luck to pull off what she's got.

* * *

When Nolan and I leave, the pride flag in the window jogs my memory about something Jason said that night in San Francisco.

"I keep wanting to ask you something," I tell Nolan. "What did your brother mean about you being there for him when he was fourteen?"

He turns his head to look at me as we walk. "I was the first person he came out to. When he was fourteen."

I do the math. When I met his brother, Nolan and I were sophomores in college, and I visited him and his family over break. We were twenty; Jason must have been fifteen then. But I didn't know he was gay. Nolan never mentioned it, nor did Jason. Not that he needed to, but it's a contrast to how open Jason is now.

"So, you were nineteen? Was that our freshman year?"

"Yeah, he came out to me when I was home for Christmas break."

As we pass an organic dry-cleaner on our way to the subway, I put it together. "Ohhh. He was out to you, but no one else?"

"For a long time, yes," he says easily—the secret he kept is no longer a secret. "At first, he didn't want anyone else to know because he was worried about what it would mean for him as an athlete. The kid lived and breathed football," Nolan says, admiration in his tone. "But he wasn't sure how he was going to manage it all—sports and, well, who he was. And he wasn't sure how our dad would react. But he needed someone to talk about it with."

"You were his person," I say, feeling all sorts of tender for the two of them, thinking of what they meant to each other. What they still mean. "I don't think I knew he was gay till we graduated from college."

"Yep. That's when he was ready for others to know," Nolan says, matter-of-factly.

That all makes perfect sense. "I'm glad he had you, Nolan. It makes me happy he did, and I'm happy, too, that you never told me. That you waited for him to be ready."

"You gotta keep your sibling's secrets," he says, bumping shoulders with me.

Don't I know it. "Callie was like that in her own way. She didn't want to tell Mom and Dad she was making plans for her bucket-list road trip. She didn't want anyone to know till we were doing it."

He tilts his head, a line creasing his brow. "Was she afraid they'd talk her out of it?"

I shake my head, absently running a finger over the ladybug necklace as we cross the street. "She just knew it was going to be harder for them to accept what it meant—the road trip, that is. The symbolism of it all," I say, fighting to keep my tone even. "The reality of it."

"You'd already accepted it," he says softly, knowing me so well.

"And I wanted her to have her trip. It was her wild childhood dream. I wanted to give it to her."

He's silent for half a block, but it's a comfortable silence, the kind we both have grown accustomed to over the years. "Did you ever read or see *The Last Lecture*?"

"I watched it on YouTube," I answer.

"That reminds me of what Randy Pausch said. 'And as you get older, you may find that "enabling the dreams of others" thing is even more fun.'"

Yes. So much yes.

That nugget of wisdom is a key turning in a lock. A door opens, and I don't feel so stupid for what I did. I get, now, what my heart realized back then.

I stop on the corner, grab his arm. "Do you know why I got an extension on my college loan?"

He shakes his head.

"I thought I could pay it off in time. I'd put aside enough to pay it off. I had six months of fashion shoot contracts coming in, and I was going to use that to pay most of the balance," I say, then begin my confession. "And instead, I used that for the road trip. I told Callie it was money from the makeup gig. Which it was, so I didn't lie to her. I just didn't tell her I'd budgeted that cash for something else. I wanted her to have her dream trip." I swallow around an ache in my throat. "So, I got an extension and used the money that was supposed to pay off my loan for travel expenses."

"You did that for her?" He sounds awestruck.

I give a *what-would-you-do* shrug. "It was her dream. How could I not?"

He smiles, and it feels like a new kind of grin, full of an even deeper understanding of me. "You couldn't."

I twist the necklace in my hand. "Am I stupid?"

"No. That's . . . beautiful, Emerson." He looks like he wants to hold me, and kiss me, and tell me all the things.

Instead, he clears his throat and drags a hand along the back of his neck. "Thanks for sharing. I'm really glad you did."

So am I. Funny, because I didn't think I'd want to tell him. I didn't think I could say that without feeling foolish.

But he made me feel the opposite. I shouldn't have been afraid. Talking, sharing, showing him the sad, scared, ugly, and weird parts of me is what I've always done.

Trouble is, I fall a little more for him every single day.

The genie is getting so much bigger than the bottle.

* * *

The next night, I head out to Jo's apartment, wearing a cute black dress and Converse sneakers, and a backpack with makeup in it.

As I step onto the elevator, a broody man looks up from his paperback. It's Max, in the flesh. He practically drips Mister Rochester vibes. I'm surprised he's not carrying the dog-eared copy of *Jane Eyre* he stepped out of. But he's reading *The Sun Also Rises*, so that tracks too.

Better to catch flies with honey, though. "Hi, Max. I'm Emerson Alva. I'm a food person too."

In slow-mo, he rakes his gaze over my face, studies me. "I know."

Okayyyy. "And I think your videos are great," I say.

He's silent for several long, weighty beats. "I suspect yours are too," he says, then nods crisply when we reach the lobby. "After you."

Weirdo.

"Have a good night," I call out, then I put the broody guy out of my mind. My brain only has room for so many men, and someone else is occupying the prime real estate.

Over at Jo's place on West Seventy-Third Street, we get dolled up for the *Tommy* revival on Broadway. I do her makeup, giving her fabulous smoky eyes and glossy lips.

"Gorgeous, babe, just gorgeous," I tell her, then spin her around and show her my work in the mirror.

She gasps. "Don't ever leave me. When I run my next auction, I want you to do my makeup too," she says, grabbing my hands, playfully begging.

"I won't even charge you, babes," I stage-whisper.

"Speaking of, when will you be wowing the New York art world with this fab collection you're working on?"

"Next month," she says, and as we finish getting ready, she gives me details of her new projects and a promotion she's applying for at her auction house. "I have an interview for it next week. Fingers crossed."

I cross mine and hold them up. "I'm proud of you, woman. You have made a name for yourself in the New York art world," I tell her as we make our way to the St. James Theater.

"I'm proud of you too, Em. Doing your thing, making it all happen." We reach Times Square, and she gazes up at the glittery lights of the marquee, beckoning us to enjoy a few hours of make-believe. "I knew I could get you here in New York at last. I manifested it and it happened."

"You're magic like that," I say as we go inside and snag our orchestra seats.

"Speaking of magic, how's everything with you and Nolan?"

It's a leading question. I sit up straight, my radar beeping. "Why do you ask?"

She points at me. "Why do you react like that?"

I groan and drop my head in my hands, then serve up my heart. "I think I've had feelings for him for a long time, Jo."

When I look up, she smiles sympathetically and rubs my shoulder. "I know you have, sweetie."

Funny, how we've had this long-distance friendship, talking on FaceTime and seeing shows together when I've been in New York, but we've rarely lived in the same city. Yet, that hasn't stopped us from forging this deep bond.

Nor has it stopped her from seeing right through to my heart. "What are you going to do about it?"

"Nothing." Saying it hurts more than it should, but then the overture swells, the music billowing throughout the theater, and I lean into the make-believe for the next few hours—something I've been doing a lot of these days.

15

FOOD AND OTHER GASMS

Nolan

Sometimes when I'm alone, I practice things I want to say to Emerson. The stupid secrets I want to share with her. The *why* of them.

"Funny you should mention loans. So, about mine . . ."

After learning what she did for her sister, I'm even more convinced my story, the reason I'm so determined to keep my head above water, makes me sound like a complete nitwit.

So, I kept it to myself when she shared with me. I keep it under wraps like I've always done. The only people who know the details are my two best buds.

I'm out for a run with them a few days after the Long Food shoot, TJ and Easton pounding the pavement alongside me in Central Park.

"You almost done paying off the loan?" TJ asks.

"Close like a horseshoe," I say.

"Good. I still can't believe you got stuck with that," he adds.

"Well, I haven't always made the best decisions."

"Who has?" Easton shrugs like it's no big deal. "But you're almost there, so that's good."

"Yeah. I just want to make the final payment and put it behind me."

"And never have to tell Emerson about it?" TJ asks pointedly.

Never tell *anyone* but these two guys. These dudes are vaults, and they are also far, far away from my family and my life in San Francisco. "It doesn't exactly scream *this guy has his shit together*," I say.

Easton shakes his head. "It says nothing about you."

"Exactly," TJ agrees. "But it bugs you that you never told her. *That does* say something about you."

I'll bite. "What does it say?"

"That you want her to know the real Nolan," he tells me plainly.

Do I, though? Probably. But do I want that as a friend? Or as something more?

I shouldn't want more with her. There's no room for it in our plans. "What I want is to move back to New York," I say as the sun climbs higher. "So, the sooner I pay it off, the sooner I can do that."

TJ goes with the subject change as we near the reservoir. "Look, I'm not saying I want to see your ugly face around here more often, but I heard from some friends about a sublease in Queens," he offers.

"Awww. I love it when you sweet talk me," I deadpan.

"And Bellamy mentioned a friend in Brooklyn who is moving out of her studio soon," Easton says, just as chill. "Not that I give a fuck if you're here either."

I plaster on a smile as we run, pretending I'm inhaling the scent of their . . . adoration. "The love, gentlemen. The love. It wafts off you two like cologne."

"And I bet it smells fantastic," TJ says.

"Seriously, though," I add. "Appreciate the hookups. I truly do."

That's the simple part. But what about Emerson? Would she stay on the East Coast if the show worked out, or bounce back and forth? Would she stay if it didn't? And what happens next?

That's the trouble.

Our fate is in the hands of a network that has its own agenda, as TJ pointed out the first night we arrived.

As my buddies chat about New York rent and other quirks of the city—last week TJ saw a dude walking a tiger on a leash in Soho—my gaze falls on a food truck setting up for the day.

Kale-ing It is the sign on the truck, and it peddles all things, well, kale. It's perfect for *How to Eat a Banana*, and I need to talk to Emerson right the fuck now.

"I gotta go." That's all I say before I pick up the pace and dash back to the hotel, breathing hard and sweating as I knock on room 1208.

Ten seconds later, Emerson answers, and my heart jackhammers. Damn, she looks pretty in the morning when she's doing her makeup and her hair is all slicked back and wet. She's wearing a T-shirt and skinny jeans, and I want to undress her and kiss her all over. And make her feel spectacular with my tongue between her legs. I bet she tastes like a dream.

And fuck me. Here I go again, thinking with my little head.

I slam the door on the dirty thoughts. Now is not the time. She has her loan. So do I.

Business. Just business.

"What if they don't pick us up at the end of this trial?" I blurt. "What if Dot and Bette win the slot? What if we're relegated to the bottom of the streaming menu? If the service doesn't promote you, you don't become the next Stanley Tucci touring Italy. You become a blip." My worry spills out in a verbal ten-car pile-up. "I can't be a blip, Emerson."

With a makeup brush in one hand, she grabs me with the other and drags me inside. "That's all true. What do you want to do?"

What I *don't* want is to be back on the cusp, scraping by, bouncing from couch to couch, crushed under debt.

I take off my glasses, pinch the bridge of my nose, and pace up and down in her room. "There are no restrictions in our contract against us doing the YouTube show, so long as we don't do the chef interviews or cover the same places." I looked over the contract with Hayes, though I'm only working this idea out now. "We've only done one or two shows for our own channel since we've been here. That's not like us, Em."

"True," she says, moving to the bed and perching on the edge. "We've been busy on the Webflix show."

"And we have to do that. And I want to do that." I pace to the window, fiddle with my glasses and slip them back on. "But I also think we need to keep doing our own thing. Even if it's hard. Even if it takes a ton of time." I meet her eyes, desperation chasing my thoughts, my plans. "We can't depend on someone else."

"I wasn't doing that," she says a little defensively.

"I wasn't saying you were," I point out. "But it's just . . . we can only trust ourselves, you know?"

"I do."

"We're the only ones who'll have our backs. We were already ticking up before Webflix called. We just need to keep that trajectory, keep the same pace. What do you think?"

I implore her, hoping like hell she'll agree. She's always been a go-getter and always wanted this future. Still, I'm tense as I wait four, five, six seconds.

Then, she smiles. "When do we get rolling again?"

I stab the air. "Right now. And I know just the place to do it."

She lifts a brow and points her makeup brush at me. "No offense, but you're kind of smelly and gross. Maybe shower first."

"Brains and beauty," I say, holding my arms out wide.

She pinches her nose. "And brutal honesty," she calls as I leave to wash off the run and make myself presentable.

Three hours later, we're sampling kale chips that are so good, so crunchy, the chef must be a wizard. How else could he make these vegan, low-cal treats taste like decadent junk food?

Don't even get me started on the kale fries.

"These fries are a nine," I announce after I taste one.

Emerson goes still with shock, then gradually unfreezes. "The man *can* bend, evidently," she says.

I just smirk. "When something's this good, it deserves a nine."

"I give them a nine point five," she says, showing me up, as she does.

And I love it.

It feels good.

We find a coffee shop to buckle down afterward, and she edits while I chit-chat with fans on social media, just like we used to.

This feels just right.

But it also feels like I'm running a race to get the girl at the finish line, only I won't ever win.

The next afternoon, as we're leaving for an evening Webflix shoot, we run into Dot and Bette outside the hotel. Dot is laughing—probably at something her bestie said—and her cheeks are streaked with red, green, and yellow paint. Her hair too. Bette is also decorated in splotches.

When they spot us, both ladies wave with bright eyes and big smiles. Damn, they are friendship goals.

"Hey, cuties," Bette says and opens her arms like she's going to hug us, then she steps back. "Oops. I'm covered in paint. Today was make pies and paintball," she says, like that makes sense.

Emerson raises a finger. "Your show is now pies and paintball?" Leave it to my friend to go straight to the obvious question.

Dot shrugs happily and adjusts her blonde hair, tucking errant strands into a bandana. "It's our new shtick, apparently. We make food and tour New York. Tomorrow, we're flipping burgers at a trendy diner and taking a helicopter over the Big Apple."

That's kind of a cool concept. "So, you're like New York tour guides for food and fun," I say, adding up the pieces.

"And then Miami and DC and so on. It's a little wild," Dot says, clearly jazzed at the new direction for their show. "We've always wanted to travel like this, so it's *super fun,* as my Evelyn would say."

"And we love it. *One hundred percent,*" Bette adds. "Also an Evelyn saying."

Evelyn pops up out of nowhere; that's her schtick. She grabs Dot's arm and tugs her toward the entrance. "We have *that* meeting in thirty minutes. You need to get out of your paintball clothes and into something—"

"Yes, yes. *Dressy and on-brand.* I know, sweets, I know," she says.

Evelyn nods to the hotel entrance. "We should get ready."

But the message is *shut up.*

Fine, fine. I get it. We're competitors now, but clearly, Webflix is making changes to both our shows.

As Emerson and I grab the train to our next stop, she gives me her big-eyed look. "Well?"

I roll my eyes. "Go ahead. Play detective. I won't stop you."

"But you won't play along?" She frowns as the subway rattles downtown, taking us to Tribeca.

"I won't. Because we just don't know."

"But they *just* might get the slot," she says. "Their show is like *Golden Girls* on tour. Everyone loves *The Golden Girls*. That's a fact."

"True, true."

"And they're getting so much more bling and fanfare from Webflix," she points out. "Even more so than Max Vespertine and the Wine Dude and the Drive-Thru Babe. But Max totally appeals to the Bourdain crowd, and Drive-Thru Babe is perfect for twenty-somethings, and the Wine Dude has the whole real guy vibe. They're all so good in their own way."

She's not wrong. But I've spent my whole life competing, albeit in my own head, with the guys in my family. Not sure I want to add contention against the lovable, crazy, foodie grannies and everyone else.

Besides, adding kerosene to this worry fire Emerson is building won't help. Maybe my role is to extinguish a few of her fears with some . . . calm.

"And we're *just* going to be okay with that," I reassure her. I reach for her hand, and . . . Fuck it.

I don't *just* squeeze it. I don't *just* give a friendly pat. I thread my fingers through hers and clasp her hand in mine.

It feels right.

It *just does,* and there's nothing more to it than that.

* * *

The Green Ant is all the weird food rage. The trendy tapas restaurant in Tribeca is known for its green ant guacamole—yes, as in made with ants—and its grasshopper tacos.

A beefy man with slicked-back hair and a passion for, well, unusual combos is the mastermind behind the new eatery. His name is Romain.

"Convince me," Emerson challenges the chef. "Pretend I'm a reluctant patron and I don't want to eat grasshoppers. But you want me to try them."

"Hand to God," Romain says, pressing his palm on the stained front of his chef whites. "You'll have a foodgasm." He sets down a long tray of appetizers for us, a dipping bowl of guacamole in the center. With a lopsided grin, he adds, "And it tastes like chicken."

"Ah, but see, that's not enticing to me either. I'm the resident vegetarian." Emerson's eyes glint playfully. "Which means I get out of eating grasshoppers on a technicality. Booyah!"

The big man pats her hand. "Don't worry, sweetheart. I've got some vegan grasshoppers right here for you." Then he dips his hand under the counter and pulls out a slate gray plate, setting it in front of her.

Her eyes pop. Whoa. Dude is good.

"You have vegan grasshoppers? Just like that? You pull them out of your pocket?"

Shock, thy name is Emerson Alva.

Romain shrugs, *no big deal* style. "Make them myself. They're like crunchy pumpkin seeds." He points to the asparagus covered in seeds and stage-whispers, "Because they are pumpkins seeds."

My fearless co-host clutches her heart like she's swooning. "Someone loves a vegetarian," she croons. "Just marry me, Romain."

The chef laughs. "I like her. She's a keeper," he tells me, and I flash her a smile.

Maybe it's even a deliberately sexy smile.

Wait—call it a knowing grin.

And that feels good. Better than good, especially when she returns it with a little bob of her shoulder, a twirl of her hair, and—best of all?—a lingering gaze that heats me up.

All her attention lasers in on me as she tries the vegan grasshoppers. And I'll take it because, at this moment, a little bit of Emerson's attention is better than nothing.

But there's a show to film. I tear my gaze away from her and turn back to Romain. "Tell us about this place. How'd you start it?"

"It's about a girl."

Emerson scoots closer. "This I have to hear."

"There was this girl in the neighborhood where I grew up. She was beautiful, and I fell in love with her from afar. But she wouldn't be seen dead with someone like me—no prospects not in her league. So, I saved up some money for a gift to show I was worthy. I gave her a box of chocolates on Valentine's Day and professed my love. And she? Well, she tossed it in my front yard and said I'd never amount to anything. That box might as well be full of chocolate-covered grasshoppers or ants. She'd never touch them." He heaves a sigh but then smiles wickedly. "I suppose I was determined to prove her wrong."

"And convinced many more than her to like grasshoppers. Very impressive revenge." I raise a hand to high-five. It takes balls to launch a restaurant to prove a snotty girl wrong.

He leaves me hanging, though, and holds up a finger. "But wait. It's not only a revenge story. There's a love story too." He stretches a meaty paw to point toward the door. "Down the street there? There's a button shop. A few years ago, I met the lady who runs it, and she's now the love of my life. And having our baby."

Emerson awws, clasping her heart. "So, revenge turns to love turns to baby makes three."

"A lucky chance, if you will," Romain says.

"I'll raise a vegan grasshopper to luck," she declares, then clasps my shoulder. "And so will this guy, since he's a keeper too."

"Yeah, sometimes luck goes your way," I say.

But I'm not looking at the chef or the camera.

I'm looking at her hand on me, where she's not letting go. I don't want her to. I want to steal this moment where we're allowed to flirt, to tease, to touch.

Maybe this is the kind of luck you make for yourself.

Like holding her hand on the train.

Like making sure we keep doing our own thing.

Like trying, then trying again.

And like enjoying this directive from the network to lean into our *je ne sais quoi.*

It's weirdly freeing. It gives me permission to enjoy this feeling in my chest, kind of warm and hazy like curling up in a cozy bed at night, like lying by a fireplace when it snows, like tangling up with sun-kissed skin on a hammock.

That's how I feel with Emerson, this woman who's been by my side through thick and thin, through ups and downs. Who hasn't ever judged me. Who's never said I'm not enough.

But this feel-good, heady sensation will fade, and I'll be left with the bills like I was before.

Focus, man. Focus.

I snap to it, pick up a chip, and taste the ant guacamole. "Holy fuck, this is hella good, dude," I say.

Romain thrusts his arms in the air. "Revenge is a dish best served with insects," he shouts.

I don't dispute him there. Those sound like words to live by.

But there are other words to live by too. Words like *work hard, look out for yourself, be smart.*

Emerson and I double down, balancing two shows. At the end of each day, I'm more tired than I've been in ages. But it's a good kind of tired that I feel deep in my bones.

Three weeks in, we head up the elevator near midnight, yawning ceaselessly. When I reach my room at last, I press my face against the door and let out an over-the-top snore.

Laughing, Emerson comes up behind me, pets my hair, and whispers, "Me too."

"That's nice," I whisper, meaning her touch.

I expect her to take her hand away, but she doesn't. Instead, she strokes down, and then she glides her fingers through my hair, running her nails along my scalp. I shudder, not tired anymore. My pulse spikes, shooting up, blasting through the roof of the hotel.

I'm on fire everywhere.

The air around me shimmers, and my desire spins sharply, intensely, then distills into one wish.

I turn around, buzzing with want. Her hand drops to her side.

"I should go," she says, a hint of regret flashing in her eyes. Is she worried she made a mistake touching me?

"You don't have to," I say.

"I do, though," she says sadly, and she wheels around, turns away, and opens her door.

My heart thumps loudly in my chest, saying *follow her*. My brain says *go to 1205*.

I picture the train, and the Long Food shoot, and the luck, and the looks, and the way she shared her secret with me on the streets of New York.

I think of all the things I haven't yet told her.

My heartbeat thrums so loudly I can't hear anything else. I cross the ten feet or so to her door, and I knock.

When she answers, her big green eyes are wide, eager.

Her lips part.

She waits.

And I speak.

"Listen, I can't stop thinking about Vegas, or you, or us. I know you don't do casual, and that we said it can't happen again. I know the show means the world to us." I pause to take a breath, then I drag my hand through my hair. "But I want to say it's really hard to be with you every second and to feel this way for you. And I don't know what to do."

With a buoyant smile, she grabs my shirt and twists the fabric. "Nolan?"

"Yeah?"

"Just shut up and kiss me."

16

YOU COULD BREAK MY HEART

Nolan

When a woman lets you know what she wants, you should give it to her.

First, I follow her command. After I slam the door closed, I grab Emerson's face and haul her close.

A hard, wet kiss comes next.

I grip her tight as I take her mouth the way she likes. The way I learned in Las Vegas.

Possessively.

I drag my thumb along her jaw, pressing roughly as I kiss her with rabid intensity. With hunger and a little hurt because she likes that.

Her noises tell me how much as I give a nibble that turns into a bite. I drag my teeth along her bottom lip, and she goes boneless in my arms. I have to band my arm around her waist, and I don't fucking mind at all. I don't mind one bit as I dig my fingers into her lower back, holding her close.

I kiss her without mercy. There's nothing soft about this locking of lips. It's all edges and corners, teeth and bones.

It's also *about fucking time.*

Then I break the kiss for a second. "Want to see you. How you look when you've been kissed by me," I rasp as I drag my hands down her face, drinking her in.

Her eyes are glossy, her lips already bruised. "How do I look?"

Like you could break my heart.

"So fucking pretty," I murmur, and I'm about to dive in for more when she slides a hand between us, then up higher.

I tilt my head. "What?"

With a soft smile, she whispers, "Glasses," then takes mine off, reaching behind her to set them on the entryway table.

"Thanks." I press my forehead to hers. "I wasn't thinking."

"Good. Let's not think. Let's not think a lot."

"Works for me," I say as I dive in for another round, kissing her mouth brutally and senselessly.

She gasps then hooks a leg around my hip, pulling me closer like that. So fiery, so clear in her need.

I'm determined to kiss her everywhere. I start my travels down the column of her throat, nipping and biting, rubbing my rough stubble against her soft skin.

"Nolan," she gasps. "Everyone will see."

I stop, press a thumb to the bloom of a bruise on the

flesh right by her collarbone. "You can cover it with makeup," I offer. I'm helpful like that.

Her green eyes twinkle with the promise of a dirty secret. "More. Just gimme more."

"So greedy," I tease, then I lick her neck, alternating open-mouthed kisses with soft and tender ones, a prelude to something darker.

When I reach her earlobe, I tug it into my mouth and bite. Hard.

"Oh God," she gasps. Her hands grapple at my waist, grabbing the loops of my jeans.

She's got a plan, it seems, because now she's unbuttoning, unzipping, and reaching for my bulge.

That feels so fucking good.

Rubbing her hand over my hard-on, she moans. "Fuck me, please." It's a desperate plea.

I wrench away from her, meet her glassy-eyed gaze. "Let me fuck you with my tongue first."

Her smile is electric and wanton.

Two minutes later, she's naked and spread out on the bed. I'm shirtless and in my new favorite place—between her thighs. As I rake my gaze over my fearless woman's beautiful body, reality hits me square in the chest.

I'm about to bury my face between my best friend's legs, and technically, I shouldn't do that.

Fuck technicalities.

Sliding my hands up her creamy flesh, I part her legs wider then dip my face to her sweetness and taste her.

She gasps.

I groan.

We move together. I lick and kiss her slick wetness, and she bucks against me. I wrap my arms under her thighs, drag her closer, and kiss her deeply.

I lap her up.

Her breath comes in fast, frenzied pants. Her hips rise up, and her hands glide down her chest as she fondles her breasts.

Holy fuck.

She's so damn sexy as she plays with herself while I eat her out. Her right hand squeezes her breast, and her left hand travels down her body, hunting for me. She threads her fingers into my hair, brings me closer to her center.

"More. Harder," she cries.

Yes, ma'am.

I kiss her harder, a little rougher too, dragging my jaw along her soft skin. She'll have some beard burn tomorrow, and I'm pretty sure that's exactly what she wants.

Then I return to her pussy, licking and sucking and drawing the swollen bundle of nerves into my mouth.

"God, yes. Ah yes. That. More. So good," she says.

We go on like that. Her one-word commands. My mouth consuming her. My tongue licking her. Her hands grabbing and clawing me.

I do my damnedest to give her everything she wants —a nip, a bite, a kiss, a hungry lick.

She's arching and thrusting, grabbing my head tighter. I can barely breathe, and that's fine by me. I'm surrounded by her scent, her need. She's close, and I'm so fucking turned on that I'm humping the bed as I flick my tongue over her just so, right there, until . . .

With a frenzied cry, she gasps, then shouts to the edge of the sky as she comes hard and beautifully on my lips.

Pleasure pounds through me. Pride, too, as I slow my pace, listening to her cues.

I brush tender post-orgasm kisses onto her thigh, then rise to my knees and rub my palm against my straining hard-on. "Want to be inside you so badly."

She finishes undressing me in a flurry, tossing my red briefs with wiener dogs on them to the floor with an appreciative whistle. Then, she grabs a condom from her nightstand and thrusts it at me. As I roll it on, she makes a fantastic decision, getting up and rearranging herself so she's standing at the edge of the bed.

Well, that's clear. I stand as she stretches her arms out along the mattress and lifts her ass. Moving behind her, I smack her cheek.

The noise she makes is so carnal it should be illegal.

Grabbing her hips, I angle her higher then slide inside. All my brain cells short-circuit. She's hot and tight and feels spectacular surrounding my cock.

I sink all the way in, savoring that moment when I fill her completely.

I breathe out hard. My mind enters a hazy, scorched land where everything is just . . . buzzy.

And druggy.

And delicious.

"You feel so good," I tell her on a low groan as I ease out, swivel my hips, then pump back in.

With an arch of her back, she lets out a long, staggered sigh. Her fingers twist in the sheets. As I thrust, she grips harder.

"More," she urges, and my God, my Emerson has a bottomless appetite for *feeling*.

For hard, hot sex.

For hurt.

For intensity.

I pick up the pace then raise a hand again and smack the outside of her thigh.

On a throaty cry, she shudders and grips the sheets so tight her knuckles whiten, pushing her face into the mattress like she can't bear it. But that won't do. I want to see her, feel her. Be connected to my woman.

My woman.

Yes, she is mine.

In all the ways.

I lower my chest to her back, still fucking, but I grab her chin. "Wanna look at you," I tell her.

She turns her face to the side.

And I want to do more than look at her. I crush my lips to hers in a messy kiss.

A kiss that's all lightning and fire as I take her and kiss her at the same damn time. Smacking her thighs, kneading her ass, kissing and fucking and feeling.

It's furious and a little out of control, our mouths sliding, bodies slamming. I'm aching to come, but I fight it off.

Need to get her there.

One more rough, dirty kiss and it flips a switch in her. Seconds later, she gasps then shivers all over. Her sounds echo in the room like the anthemic chorus in a rock song. She hits the highest note and falls to pieces under me in a coda of incoherent murmurs and sighs.

My climax slams into me, hitting me all at once. It's everywhere as I shudder through the blissful sensations, ones I want to experience again and again.

With her.

The next day, and the next.

And every single day after that.

17

FLASH MOBS AND RECLUSIVE CHEFS

Emerson

I once told Nolan I don't do casual sex because I don't know how to act afterward.

Right now, I *do* know how to act because there is sex and then there is intimacy, and that was both.

So I don't have to act at all. I can just be . . . *me.*

Nothing felt casual about sleeping with Nolan. Thirty minutes later, I'm still basking in the afterglow as I slide my arms into a robe and tie it tightly.

"Robes are cool," I say with a sexy little jut of my hip as I leave the bathroom, post-shower.

"Maybe on you," Nolan says, hooking the towel around his waist.

I flop down on the bed, and he joins me.

Perhaps this is when the awkwardness sets in. I can

feel it creep up on me, but I swat it away with words. "Are you going to spend the night?"

He strokes his chin as if deep in thought. "It's a long way back to my place. I don't really want to do the walk of shame," he says, and I swat him.

Then I snuggle into my pillow. "I think I'm a pervert."

He laughs, drops a kiss to my neck, chases it with a nibble. "Why's that?"

"Hello? You should know. Every time we sleep together, I'm like *more, please, bite me, hurt me, smack me.*"

He laughs. "God, it's so awful. A woman who knows her mind."

I turn to him, running a hand over a messy lock of his hair, tucking it behind his ear. He's all warm and lovely right now, all boyfriend-y.

I can't see him as just a friend any longer, or just a business partner.

My heart somersaults.

And my big mouth can't stay shut.

"What are we doing?" I mince no words, meeting his gaze straight on.

"Debating where to sleep," he says with a hint of a grin.

"Yes, I'm clear on that," I say.

He tugs at the robe's belt. "Well, if you take this dumb robe off, I can curl up with you, and we can sleep. Or not sleep," he says, waggling his eyebrows. But before I can ask again, he presses a soft kiss to the shell of my ear. "We're doing . . ."

I wait for him to finish, my pulse slamming against my skin.

"I guess what we're doing is figuring out just how terrible your taste in men is," he says with a wry smile.

I roll my eyes then close them, feeling a little hollow. If he can't say what he wants, there's no way *this* can become what I crave.

The mattress shifts. It dips near my face. Nolan's weight is on me, and I open my eyes to stare up at a hunk of a man straddling me.

"I don't know what we're doing," he says, "but I want to do it again. And it's not just the sex I want . . . It's you."

My whole body goes shivery. That's enough. Truly enough for me now. "Stay the night, please," I say again.

"You couldn't kick me out if you tried."

* * *

Talk about blue.

I stare at my neck in the bathroom mirror. My neck is the color of an alpine lake.

My phone buzzes on the counter with a text from Nolan.

Are you ready? We're cutting it close, and I know you won't want to miss the cereal.

I love cereal with a passion, but I also need to deal with this evidence.

Five minutes! Meet you downstairs.

I lean closer to the mirror, swiping on more foundation, then more powder over the mark. Almost gone. But I can't resist. I press a finger to the center of it, and sensation rushes through me.

An aftershock—maybe the reverberations from last night.

I set my hands on the vanity, close my eyes, and let the images rush in. Sex isn't everything, but it sure is something.

When you finally have the sex you long for, the kind that makes you feel like yourself, it's so hard to imagine that ending.

But there's so much more at stake.

When I open my eyes, I run my fingers over the ladybug charm. "What would you do?" I ask softly, wishing my other half would answer. Wishing I could turn to her.

My throat tightens, so I take a deep, calming breath and concentrate on finishing my makeup.

My phone pings again once I'm done. This time, it's Jo.

I have my interview today! Wish me luck.

I write back. *Sending you all the ladybug luck in the world.*

An elevator ride later, I'm scanning for a sign of Nolan when a voice rumbles past my ear.

"Good morning, Emerson Alva."

I turn to say hello to Max. He's holding a demitasse of espresso. His dark gaze searches my face. Could the man be more intense? I'd guess a resounding, gong-clanging no.

"Hi, Max. How's everything going?"

"Well," he answers in between sips, pinky up. "Incredibly well. I'll be interviewing Raven at La Fontaine today."

Shut the front door. "He's like the Banksy of chefs. Raven hardly does any interviews."

Max holds up his free hand, waggling one finger. "His interview with me is the first he's done in years."

Wow. "That's big time. Good on you."

He gives a crisp nod. Then his eyes dip to my collarbone—just a moment before he jerks them back up. "I trust it's the same for you."

Without waiting for my answer, he turns on his Doc Martens and walks the other way.

No, dude, I'm not hanging out with reclusive three-Michelin-star chefs who've given zero interviews. I'm eating cereal shakes and grading Froot Loops pancakes.

With a deep breath, I spin around, shaking my head, and nearly walk into Evelyn.

And Dot.

And Bette.

My God, it's a food show contestant convention this morning. "Hi, Dot. Hi, Bette. Have they got you leading a Times Square tour today?" Because they're both wearing *I Love NY* shirts.

"Yes! And supposedly, there's going to be a flesh mob for us," Dot says.

Evelyn rolls her eyes. "Flash mob."

"Yes, that."

Webflix is rolling out the red carpet for them. And for Max. "That sounds wild," I say, trying to sound legit buzzed for them.

I am happy for them.

Of course I am.

Dot leans, her eyes widening, then she inches closer to me. "Sweetie, you missed a teeny, tiny spot," she whispers, then points gently to my bruise. "Might want to get a touch more powder."

My cheeks pinken. "Thanks."

I spot Nolan lounging on a couch, chatting with Marcos. I give him the sign for *I'll be right back,* then I scurry to the ladies' room, grab some powder from my backpack, and paint over the evidence of last night.

When I finish the work, I stuff my makeup back into my bag, but my hands are shaking, my breathing shallow.

I try to let go of the worries.

I want to stop worrying. Truly, I do.

But I also just *want.*

I want to pay off the loan. I want to do right by Callie. I want to stay friends with Nolan. I want to be his lover. I want our show to succeed. I want it to succeed *for him,* most of all. I know that man—know his needs and his secret hopes. I want to fulfill them all for him.

This all seems too much to ask.

I stuff my concerns down to the bottom of my bag, cover them up, and put on a grin.

In the lobby, I find my co-host and the Wine Dude. "Hey, Marcos," I say to the bearded fellow.

"Hey Em," he says. "Let me know if the Cinnamon Life low-cal milkshake is all that. I've been jonesing to try it."

"I'm sure it'll go great with a Merlot," I say stupidly. Since what I really want to say is *How are they wooing you today? Tell me everything.*

Marcos just gives me a *that was a strange response* look, then smiles kindly on his way out.

"You okay?" Nolan asks, guiding me outside to a waiting Lyft. As I get in, I catch a glimpse of Marcos sliding into a sleek black town car.

My stomach craters.

"No," I say, with a gulp.

Nolan climbs in and shuts the door, then he takes my hand in his, covers it. "What's wrong, honey?"

Oh God.

Honey.

Nothing is wrong now.

Everything is butterflies.

I dip my chin, my hair curtaining my face. He brushes it back, cups my jaw, and gently turns me toward him. "What's wrong?" he asks again.

"I just . . ."

"You're worried everyone else is doing better?"

I nod. "It's stupid. It's so stupid."

"It's not," he says, then presses a kiss to my forehead. "But you have to try to let it go. Okay?"

I nod, a little shaky. "I just want it, though. For us. For you."

His eyes do something I've never seen before. They tighten with something like pain.

"Are *you* okay?" I ask, turning the question back on him.

He takes off his glasses and pinches the bridge of his nose. "I will be."

I sense there's something he wants to tell me, but the car pulls up to the cereal joint. It's time to focus on the job and not on this kernel of worry that's sprouting and digging roots inside me.

18

COMPLEX MATH

Nolan

I can't keep a stupid secret from Emerson any longer. After she declares the cereal shake a nine point two and I give it a six, I grab her elbow and guide her to Abingdon Square Park, a triangular patch of grass and playground at the edge of Chelsea, a secret in the middle of the city that never sleeps. Abingdon Square Park feels like New York is breathing quietly, away from the restless masses.

We sit on a green slatted bench, and I turn to Emerson. "I don't owe money on a student loan," I say.

She tilts her head, her eyes question marks. "What do you mean?"

I blow out a breath. My bones tighten like I'm a Jack-in-the-box. It's a little painful, but after what she said in the car—*I just want it, though, for us, for you* —I know TJ and Easton were right. It's time.

"I don't have student loans for cooking school," I begin, trying to release the strangling tension.

A line burrows into her forehead. "I know that. You've told me Jason wanted to pay for it. I thought you had a small student loan from college. That your dad wanted you to pay for some of college," she says. Her face is a complex math equation. Mine is probably a portrait of shame.

I wince to hear my lie repeated back to me. "That's not true," I admit.

She blinks. "Oh. Okay."

"My dad is, well, you know. He's well-off. So's Jason."

She nods. "Right."

I rub a hand along my chin. "I don't owe anything from college. I . . . made that up."

Emerson jerks back her head. "What?"

Hell, this is harder than I thought. "I lied to you. I didn't want to tell you, or them, the truth."

"Nolan, you're freaking me out. What is it?"

"The bistro I opened with Inés? In France?"

"Yes?"

"She put up most of the initial cash, but I helped with the rest. Used basically all my savings. And I co-signed on her loan. When we split up, she said she'd cover the payments," I say.

Emerson sighs sadly, easily doing the math now that she has the numbers. "She didn't take over?"

I shake my head. "A few months ago, she defaulted

on the loan I co-signed. That's how I ended up with the debt for her failed restaurant."

Her expression falters; her jaw falls open. "Oh, Nolan," she says, soft and sympathetic.

But I don't deserve sympathy. "It's embarrassing."

She reaches for my face, cups my cheeks. "Don't. Don't be embarrassed. I get it."

"You do?"

"You didn't tell me because you had to keep it from your dad and Jason. Because they'd pay the debt, and you didn't want that. So, you kept it to yourself." She clasps my face tighter. "Am I right?"

My heart spasms. How the hell did she figure that out? "You *are* a detective," I whisper.

She shakes her head. "No. I just know you. I get you."

"You do," I say, then tell the rest of the story. Now that I've started, I can't stop. "They didn't like her. They told me not to move. Not to follow her. They were right. I didn't want to disappoint them. And I guess I didn't want to disappoint you either."

"I'm not disappointed. And I won't be. Ever," she says gently. Then, she lets go of my face like she just realized she was holding me.

"You don't have to stop," I offer.

A soft laugh falls from her lips. "Is that so?"

"That is so," I say, then take a beat. "You're not pissed I lied?"

She rolls her eyes. "I didn't tell you the truth about my loan. Why on earth would I be mad you didn't either?"

"But yours was for something good, something noble," I point out.

"Maybe yours was for something good too. Self-preservation," she says with a knowing shrug. "But I'm glad you told me."

I'm glad I did too. I just didn't expect her reaction, the purity of it, or that it would make me fall a little harder for her.

Trouble is, I also want to protect her from guys like me.

Guys who can't give her everything she deserves.

19

THE TRUTH OF TERRIBLE TASTE

Emerson

As we leave the park, Nolan asks if I want to take the afternoon off.

The idea sounds brilliant. "I do."

"No shop talk," he commands.

I mime zipping my lips.

We walk around Chelsea, then catch a subway uptown, and stop at The Met before turning around and deciding art isn't our speed.

Instead, we wander through Central Park, stopping at Bethesda Terrace and staring at the New York skyline. "Did you ever think about putting New York on your road trip?" Nolan asks.

I shake my head. "Callie never liked New York. She loved all things vintage and retro. She wanted to see the places you'd visit on a great American bucket-list road trip. But I like New York. It suits me."

"Because to really succeed here requires a ton of preparation and life hacks, and you're amazing at that?"

I laugh. "Because New York is kind of a jerk, and I can be one too."

His eyebrow arches with doubt. "I'm not really sure you are."

I growl at him and narrow my eyes. "Don't you dare say I'm nice."

"You're kind of nice sometimes, Emerson."

I pretend I'm going to jump him, wrapping my arms around his neck in a faux headlock. He laughs then drops a kiss onto my nose. So, it's like that. We kiss in public now. My stomach does a loop-de-loop. Boyfriend-y indeed.

But I don't want to label this just yet. It's too risky, too new. I don't even know how we can pull it off, or whether we should.

I'd rather linger in this glowy state for a little longer.

"But seriously. Sometimes I wonder if that's why my relationships haven't worked out," I muse as I let go of him. "If I speak my mind too much."

He tosses his head back, cackling. "Em, your relationships didn't work out because you've had terrible taste in men. Would you like me to go through and present the evidence?"

"By all means. This should be a real character assassination," I say, but in my head, thoughts are racing. Do I have terrible taste? Is that a thing?

"First, there was Topher. He brought his friends on a

date with you. His fraternity brothers," Nolan says, and I groan at the horrible memory.

I defend myself. "And I didn't go out with him again."

Nolan clears his throat. "You saw him one more time."

Ugh. Busted. "I believed in second chances," I grumble, looking out at the lake.

"And then there was super-boring useless-fact guy. The one who tried to scare you off roller coasters."

"We already agreed about that one," I say, faking a huff, but something nags at me—the start of an answer to the terrible taste question.

"And then there was that dude. What was his name? Paul? Larry? Bob? And it turned out he was just kind of creepy. He would show up on your doorstep unannounced."

I shudder at the memory and concede, "Fine. Fine. You're right. I have terrible taste."

Nolan strokes his chin, gives me an intense stare through those glasses. "Now, tell me, why do you think you have such terrible taste in men?" he asks in a German accent, affecting an old-school therapist vibe.

The uncomfortable idea starts to color itself in. A reason, perhaps, or the beginning of one that I don't quite like.

So, I deflect. "I suppose it all goes back to my childhood," I say, as if I'm on a shrink's couch. Then, I answer him with a piece of the truth. "But it doesn't make sense. My parents have a good marriage. They're still together. Callie had a couple good relationships. I've had good examples. I don't really know why I'm drawn to men who are wrong for me. Men I don't see a future with."

But the sketch becomes clearer, the lines drawn in. Is it because I've carried a torch for this guy all along?

Or . . .

Wait.

Is there some other reason? Something deeper, something that I've pushed down even further?

My chest constricts. My airways tighten, and for several seconds, the world spins, like I'm suffocating.

No matter what, no matter why, this romance with Nolan won't end the way I want. I'll lose someone I love again.

I try to shake away the thoughts, to stuff them down again. I throw the spotlight away from me and onto him. "What about your taste? Inés was bad news," I say.

"As we discussed earlier today."

"So, you're the same. You have terrible taste too!"

"Present company excluded," he says with a soft smile and a poignant gaze that settles my anxious mind a little.

Especially because he says it so easily, then sighs as he watches boaters skim across the lake. "I think with Inés it seemed like we had so much in common. I guess that's why you shouldn't mix business and pleasure," he says, turning to me, those hazel eyes serious. "But then, that's not why it didn't work out with her."

"You loved her. It hurt when you learned she abused that trust."

"I did. I felt pretty stupid," he admits. "Maybe that's

the other reason I didn't tell you about the money. I didn't want to remind myself of that bad choice."

I rub his shoulder, squeezing it. "Do you think that's why you haven't been serious with anyone since then?"

"I've dated here and there," he protests, but it's feeble.

"You're a serial monogamist, but you never go that far. As far as with Inés," I point out.

"Who wants to get hurt again?" he asks, offhand.

Maybe we're both afraid—for different reasons, but valid ones. "No one *wants* to get hurt. But that shouldn't stop you from trying," I say.

Maybe that's advice I should follow myself.

As the afternoon spills into evening, I vow to do just that. To let Nolan in. To let go of some of my fear, even though I'm not quite sure which I'm afraid of—that I've been falling for my best friend all my adult life, or that I won't let myself fall.

I don't know the answer, so I indulge in the physical, hoping it'll bring me closer to understanding.

Soon, we're back at the hotel. Twilight falls over the city, and in my room, we strip down to nothing. Last night, I wanted the intensity, the press of his fingers on my skin, the feel of his teeth on my body. Right now, I want all of him against me, so I pull Nolan onto the bed and hand him a condom.

Tonight, I let myself revel in the bliss of the moment, in the strange and wonderful sensation of making love with my best friend.

Of feeling him deep inside me.

Of relishing his delirious kisses along my neck, his warm skin pressed to mine, his words in my ear.

"What am I going to do with you?" he whispers.

Keep me. Keep me.

I don't want us to stop. I want it all. I want everything.

But I can foresee the future. All I can do is savor the press of him against me, the feel of his pulse thundering in time with mine, and the insistent hum in my heart and my head.

The hum that tells me I might be in love.

That tells me this won't end well.

* * *

In the morning, I get a text from Jo—a sad face, chased with a sadder message. *I'm leaving New York and moving to London.*

I gasp.

Impossible! I thought she'd be in New York forever!

The day is full of shoots and food and cameras and work, but that evening I march into Gin Joint intent on getting to the bottom of this blasphemy. Jo is perched on a couch and holding a glass of wine, looking smart in a yellow blouse, her hair blow-dried. The sharp effect, though, is muted by her frown.

When I reach her, I park my hands on my hips. "I refuse to accept this."

"Me too."

"Why are you leaving?"

"My company is relocating. They're shutting down

the New York office. The job I want? The VP promotion? It's in London now."

I sink onto the blue velvet chaise and drape an arm around her. "That is not okay. We're finally in the same city. I don't want you to go."

She lays her head on my shoulder, her brown hair spilling onto my chest. "Just handcuff me to New York, please." Jo sounds as unenthusiastic as I feel.

"Do you want to leave?"

Lifting her face, she shakes her head, her blue eyes brimming with wistfulness. "It sounds like a great opportunity. Most art curators would chomp at the bit for a job in the UK. But London is full of . . ."

"Bad memories?" I supply, knowing her story well.

"Yes. Too many of those." She reaches for me and squeezes my hand. "Plus, all my friends are here. I know you don't live here yet, but I was going to keep you in town. We would all hang out together, all the time. You and Nolan, TJ and Easton. All of us."

That sounds like the life I desperately want.

"I'm going to miss you." My voice wobbles as I slump deeper into the couch.

A server swings by and asks if I want something. "Your saddest white, please," I reply.

He smiles. "I've got an uplifting Chardonnay. Will that do?"

With a heavy sigh, I nod. When he brings the drink a few minutes later, I lift my glass in a toast to Jo. "To me, kicking and screaming and not wanting to let you go."

"To me, kicking and screaming and not wanting to leave," she says.

As we clink glasses, realization hits me. I've only been in New York for a few short weeks, but already it's where I want to stay. True, I miss Katie and my friends in San Francisco. But I feel at home here. I feel like myself here.

New York seems like the starting over I didn't know I needed.

"I love this city," I confess to Jo. "I want to stay. I just hope I can."

Jo grabs my hand, squeezes. "You and New York seem like a good pair. You're both so tough."

"I don't feel so tough when everything can change on a dime."

"I won't argue with you there," she says.

We drink again, both a little lost with how quickly our lives are changing. Then, she taps her fingers on my leg. "So . . . what's going on with you and Nolan?"

Before I've even begun to explain, the door of the bar swings open and the guys come in, joining us. An impromptu quintet of friends.

Over the years, the five of us have moved around, but we've always found our way back to each other, through college, and after college, through work, and amidst all the ups and downs of adulting.

Now we're together once more, but not for long. Jo's taking off. Me, I'm roosting here for perhaps the first time.

As for me and my best guy friend, I have no idea what happens next with us. If he's returning to San Francisco, and whether we're staying or going. Most of all, whether I'll let myself feel, truly feel, all the emotions storming inside me, or if the painful prospect of hoping so hard and so futilely for a different future will stop me.

Or maybe, I realize, he'll stop us before I can.

Because Nolan doesn't sit next to me, or hold my hand, or kiss me.

I try not to read too much into that. But as we reassure Jo that we'll stay in touch no matter what, that friendships these days can transcend geography and oceans, I keep thinking about change.

How you can plan.

How you can learn.

How you can watch every how-to video on YouTube, but none of them can prepare you for what it means to lose a sister, to chase a dream, and most of all, to fall in love.

To fall in love and figure out what you're willing to risk for it.

20

MIDNIGHT MEETINGS

Nolan

The next morning, Emerson rounds up the crew once again with a group text to TJ, Easton, and me.

We're bringing Jo cinnamon rolls for breakfast, and we're going to help her pack. Be there at nine or give up your friend card forever.

Seconds later, our group thread is full of *obvs* and *I'll be there* responses. An hour later, Jo's apartment is full of the lot of us bearing mini cinnamon rolls, hugs, and promises we'll stay in touch while she's across the pond.

When Emerson pops open the purple box she brought, Jo rubs her palms together. "Oh, look. It's Emerson's booty."

I give my co-host's ass a leer. I know how it feels in my hands and against my palm when I smack it. Know, too, how much she likes a swat or three or four.

It's a bit of a miracle that I can say drily, "It is a nice one."

Jo bonks me on the shoulder. "Booty as in plunder. Food plunder. Baked goods."

"Prizes, riches, loot," TJ puts in, then adds, "At least, that's how I *sometimes* use the word."

The five of us joke some more, down coffee, eat sweets. Jo's a touch cheerier than she was last night, but not much. "I'm going to miss you all so much."

Emerson frowns then pulls Jo in for a hug. "I'm going to miss you too."

Is it even harder for Emerson, because of her sister, when someone leaves? It must be.

After we help Jo pack, the rest of us fan out. TJ heads to a coffee shop to work on his book—or, as he says, *attempt to drain words from his beleaguered brain*—and Easton departs to his office for work. Emerson and I make our way to an afternoon shoot.

On the way there, I venture, "It's hard for you because of Callie, right?"

Her brow furrows. "Jo leaving?"

"Yeah. Is that part of why it's hitting you so hard?" I ask as we walk.

She hums as if considering the idea. "You're probably right. I don't think I realized that. Which is, maybe, silly of me."

"No, it's not." But maybe I shouldn't have tried to psychoanalyze this moment. "I didn't mean to bring up something hard," I say.

She grabs my arm. "I'm glad you did. I think you're right. It probably is harder. Also, I was truly looking forward to spending time with Jo while we were here in New York—going to shows, getting a drink, and just hanging out. And now we can't do that. I don't like it when people leave," she says, then smiles like *you've figured me out*.

"I think that's reasonable," I say.

I want to promise I won't leave her.

More than anything, I want to promise her that.

Maybe someday I can.

* * *

The next night, after an evening shoot at a swank new supper club, Emerson and I are signing T-shirts and taking pics with fans, when from the end of the line, a redhead shouts, *"Foodgasm!"*

The woman squeals when she meets Emerson. "I have been watching your show forever. Back when you did it with your sister," she gushes.

Emerson's green eyes twinkle. "You're a longtime fan, then," she says, kind of in awe.

"I am. And I did not think I would like it with someone else. Took me a while to warm up to him." She points to me.

Emerson loops her arm around my shoulders. "I get that. He's a tough one to like," she says with a wink.

I curl my arm around her waist and squeeze her hard. "Same for her."

The redhead smiles. "But I'm glad you guys started the show again. It's just so fun. I look forward to every new episode alert."

"And we love doing it," Emerson says.

That right there reminds me why a promise not to leave Emerson is hard, if not impossible, to make. We are so wrapped up in each other—how can I make a promise when the stakes are so high?

But when we're finished and we board the subway toward the hotel, Emerson leans her head on my shoulder and whispers, "Would you knock on my door at midnight?"

I give her a questioning look. Lately, I just go over whenever. "Sure. Why?"

"I just want that."

And I want to give her what she wants. I'll deal with promises another time.

* * *

As the clock ticks the last minutes of that day, I knock on her door. She swings it open wearing only red lace panties. Nothing else.

I groan savagely at the sight.

She presses her finger to her lips, then grabs the waistband of my jeans. She tugs me into the room, over to the wall, and pushes me against it.

"Shh," she whispers.

I don't plan on saying a word. My dick's already reporting for duty, ready for whatever plan Emerson has in store.

She reveals her intentions as she unzips my jeans then sinks to her knees. After urging my pants down my thighs, she stops, pressing her face to the fabric of my boxer briefs and rubbing her cheek against my straining hard-on.

And the panda design on them. "Nice pandas," she says.

"They look even better off," I say.

With a wicked gaze, she looks up at me. Her eyes are eager. She pulls my boxer briefs down, freeing my cock. Her breath comes in a rush as she stares at my dick. Then she dips her face. Swirls her tongue. Laps me up.

"Oh fuck," I grunt.

This isn't the first time she's taken me in her mouth. But it's the first time she's done it like this—me against the wall, her in control. She grabs my right hand, guides it to the back of her neck, and curls it around. My muscles shake. My dick hardens even more.

A zap of pleasure singes my spine as she licks me again then whispers, "Don't move."

I will do anything she asks. "I won't," I murmur, so damn curious what she's got in mind.

She shows me, opening her mouth and drawing me in, first an inch, then another. When I'm halfway in, I can feel her throat working. Saliva pools around my cock, and she breathes in, trying to relax her throat. Then she guides her mouth onto my cock farther, farther.

Holy fuck.

My skin sizzles.

Emerson's lips stretch wide and wonderfully around my dick, her mouth closing in on the base.

I am there, all the way in, and this is the best midnight treat ever. My hand tightens around her neck.

She nods in encouragement, telling me to grip her harder. I do, curling my fingers roughly around her skin. Her shoulders rise, give a sexy little shudder.

Then she slides her hands around me, grabbing my ass and tugging.

A signal.

"Honey," I murmur. "Are you sure?"

Her eyes say *please.*

"You want me to fuck your face?"

A moan against my shaft. A glossy look in her green irises.

And I oblige, giving her what we both want. A thrust, then I ease out. She gasps, I push back in. She squeezes my ass, her fingernails digging in. I grip her neck harder, pressing against her flesh.

"You good?"

She nods wildly.

And I fuck her mouth like that—as a slick of saliva slides down her chin, as she gags but refuses to let go, urging me deeper with her hands. As I pump, pleasure accelerates with every thrust.

I warn her when I'm about to blast off. She digs her nails into my ass one more time, and my world spirals into filthy bliss as I come down her throat.

It's insane and wild and intimate, beautiful in its own dirty way.

Then, it gets even better when she grabs my hand, pushes me onto the bed, and crawls up my chest. "Can I fuck your face?"

"You fucking better," I tell her as she sheds her panties.

When she rides my face as wildly as I fucked hers, I'm sure I want to find a way to keep her.

And it's not for the sex—this deeply intimate, amazingly passionate sex.

What I want might also be the way to get it—its own solution if I can just work out the puzzle.

21

TA-TA FOR NOW

Emerson

A few days later, I'm still a little sore in all the good ways. Along my hips. On my ass cheeks. Between my thighs.

The bruises ache beautifully.

They make me *feel* in ways I haven't before. They make me think about things I didn't want to consider.

Like how the hell to lifehack my way into Nolan's heart without confronting the uncomfortable reality of my so-called terrible taste.

Only, probably not this second since Ilene emailed last night and requested a check-in. Like that's not foreboding at all.

Part of the contract calls for regular meetings, so let's get regular!

We said yes, of course. We'll see her, finish our

shoots over the next week, then what? Do we return to San Francisco and wait? Check out of our swank hotel, then couch surf while we stay here and shoot videos for our YouTube channel?

It feels like limbo.

I could convince Jo to let me sublease her place, but I'm not in her income bracket. I can't ask her to take a hit on rent for me.

There are too many what-ifs.

But this is a fact—we're meeting Ilene, and it's time to camouflage my collarbone again.

Once I've blended foundation and powder over my bites, I meet up with Nolan downstairs, and we hustle out of the hotel to check in with Ilene before our shoot today. Melt My Heart, where we're filming today, is a specialty sandwich shop that supposedly has the most orgasmic grilled cheese anywhere.

Well, good grilled cheese *is* toe-curling.

A few blocks away, the pink-haired executive waits for us at the counter of an austerely black-and-white café called Good Morning. She points to the menu with her particular vim and vigor. "I tested this place yesterday, and it is the best! Good Morning only serves turmeric beverages, and turmeric is one of the foods that will change your life. You must try the Straight Turmeric Morning Blast-Off. It's life-changing," she says.

"Thanks, but I just had a coffee," Nolan replies, all deadpan and mischief.

He beat me to it again. I shoot daggers at him with my eyes.

"But I'm sure Emerson would love one," he adds with the sweetest smile.

I glare harder. I might torture him with my mouth later, licking and sucking but refusing to draw him all the way in for a good, long time.

Wait, that doesn't sound like torture, except maybe the most exquisite kind.

Ilene spins toward me, her big eyes imploring. "Emerson, join me. You have to. Pretty please? I insist." She presses her palms together.

"Sure. I'll do a turmeric latte," I say, plastering on a smile. *Yay, I get to drink gross coffee blends.* Maybe the milk and foam will mask the disgusting taste. A woman can hope.

A few minutes later we grab a table, though it's more like a seat on a concrete slab at a concrete bar. Good Morning takes "stark" to new levels. Nolan and I sit next to each other across from the woman who holds the fate of our career in her hands.

Ilene riffles in her purse for a gleaming silver metal straw, which she raises in victory before dropping it in her tumbler. She sips some straight turmeric smacking her lips in satisfaction.

I smile as I lift the white mug, bracing myself for the hell of a turmeric latte. *Yum.* Ilene beams, her white teeth gleaming.

"So, everything is going great. Super great. We love what you're doing. Just keep doing it," she says.

That's nice but a little vague. "Is there anything you want us to change?" I ask.

Nolan jumps in to ask, "More interviews? Less interviews? Do you want more focus on New York? Different types of places? We can go divey or upscale, food truck or pop-up—we've got a long list of spots."

Ilene nods thoughtfully, taking another sip. "Interesting, very interesting."

Umm. What's interesting? Which one? I don't want to put her off, so I toss out more ideas. "I've always thought it would be fun to give tips on surviving dinner parties," I begin.

Her eyes twinkle, saying *go on*.

"Like a funny little segment on how to make small talk when the guest next to you can only talk about traffic or the weather," Nolan adds. We brainstormed this concept together. "Or project management software."

We agreed project management software is *trés* boring.

"Yes! That happened to me the other night," Ilene says. "Dinner parties are straight from Sartre. As in, *hell is other people*." Ah, so she's a philosophical health nut. Truly, this city takes all people. "Though, *supposedly* Sartre said his quote was misunderstood. Or so my dinner party partner told me. Whatevs! I say he got it from some *other* dinner party."

Maybe we're onto something. "So, that could be a fun addition," I say, hoping to capture more of her enthusiasm. "Along with more of the judging, maybe even getting audiences involved. Possibly some of the red-carpet treatment, too, like the others are getting."

Another sip, another nod. "Audience involvement. I

just love it," she says, sounding like I proposed inventing gravity when it didn't exist before.

"Should we sketch out some of those ideas?" Nolan asks, as eager as I am. "Try to work them into the show?"

"Nah! Just keep doing what you're doing," she says, then checks her watch. She takes one more sip. "Gah. Gotta go. I've got an appointment at Saks." She jumps up. "TTFN."

Then, she vanishes like a superhero, disappearing out of the café in a flash of pink hair and rocket fuel.

I stare at Nolan, my heart an anvil. "She couldn't even take time for 'ta-ta for now,'" I say forlornly.

He smiles softly. "It's fine."

"Is it, though? Jo is leaving, and Ilene gave us less than four minutes of her time. I just feel like we're falling behind. Don't you?"

"Sometimes," he says, his eyes gentle. "But I'm trying to enjoy what we have."

We as in him and me, or *we* as in the show? That's what I should ask, but I'm too afraid of the answer.

"So, what do we do?" I grab his arm, squeezing his hard bicep. I want to gift wrap our chances with a big red bow, and that's just dumb. But I want what I want. "What do we do to win?"

"We might not, Emerson. We might just have to be happy with what we have," he says, the calm in the center of my storm.

Like he's always been.

He's my point of balance. My safe harbor.

My heart goes smushy at the thought. But still, I

want so much. I want this success so deeply. I want it for him. "Nolan, what if—"

He leans in and silences me with his mouth.

When his soft, firm lips cover mine, the world spins away. My head goes pleasantly blank, my body delightfully warm and tingling.

And I give in.

To whatever we can be.

Nolan wraps a hand around my head, curling his fingers through my hair. He slips his tongue into my mouth, deepening our connection, pulling me closer as he kisses me in a very public display of affection, giving me a very not-safe-for-work kiss. With the sweep of his mouth, I forget everything except the taste of his lips, the scent of his skin, and the way I feel when I'm in his arms.

Safe. Safe and thrilled, all at once.

Questions flick through my head. Will audiences like the mystery of us if we're no longer a mystery? What if there's no more what-if? And the biggest one of all—will I let myself have *this*?

But logic is hard to locate when he's shutting me up with a kiss like he knows me, cares about me, and wants me.

Evidently, sometimes I just need kissing.

When he breaks away, I don't have any more answers to the career questions, but I'm coming closer to the personal one.

I'm inching nearer to understanding my walls—and maybe how to scale them.

Let go of the past. Say goodbye to the things I clutch

too tightly. Release my guilt. I want to tell Nolan I think I finally know why I've had terrible taste.

"Nolan . . ." I try to say more, but the words stick, and I look away from his hazel eyes to catch my breath. I'm still so dizzy from his lips I can't form thoughts into words.

So dizzy that it takes a few blinks to register who it is smirking down at me.

Max Vespertine.

22

MELT OR BREAK

Nolan

This guy.

His smug face is the last thing I want to see. I don't want to watch his lips curl in slow motion, painful milliliter by more painful millimeter, into a slick grin.

Max points a long finger at the table where Emerson and I sit. "Ilene left her straw. She asked me to fetch it."

My face reddens, cheeks flaming. I can't believe we were busted by this Bourdain copycat who thinks he's the shit.

I grab the straw, thrust it at him. "Here you go. Wouldn't want her to be without it," I say, cool as all the cucumbers in the summer salads in this city.

"She does love her straws," Max says, still smiling like a pussycat.

I steal a glance at Emerson. Her face reads *Oh hell, oh fuck, oh no.*

In spite of the horror on her face, her eyes say she's dying to know if Max is going to Saks with Ilene. Sounds like a Dr. Seuss book, and as much as it pains me, I fall on that sword for Detective Emerson. "Have fun at Saks," I remark evenly, like he didn't just score a juicy are-they-or-aren't-they secret to clutch in his paws.

"Yes. Shopping. It's a thing," Max says.

Somehow, I don't roll my eyes. It's hard but I manage.

"Yup. It sure is."

He puffs out his chest, stands a little taller. "So, this has been quite interesting." His dark eyes shift from Emerson to me and back as if adding up the evidence.

"It's very interesting," I say evenly.

Dude, you saw the evidence. It's not complicated. Now make yourself scarce.

"And on that note," Max says with one more knowing glance our way, "I'm off." He strolls to the door, looks back over his shoulder, and zings, "Oh, and best of luck."

When he's finally gone, Emerson blows out the biggest breath in the city.

"Nolan," she says, her tone stretched thin, her face mired in worry.

I know what to do. I hate it, but it's the only choice.

"Em," I begin heavily, feeling like I'm ripping off a piece of my heart. "I think we should cool it."

She freezes. Silence consumes her for several terrible seconds until her voice trembles, "You do?"

I hate myself, but this is necessary. I grab her hand under the table and squeeze it. "There's too much at stake. I don't trust that guy. We're not doing anything wrong, but what if Hayes is right? What if Ilene meant it when she covered her ears that day we met and said she didn't want to know? What if the mystery is what sells our show?"

Her lower lip quivers, but she nods. She's so damn tough, even as her eyes shine with tears. She nods again, several times, then tugs her hand out of mine.

My hand is cold without hers, my heart hollow.

"Of course," she says.

"Just because . . . it's too risky. We both want—"

"I know," she says, a bit sharp.

Sharper than I expected.

That stings too, but I deserve it. I should be telling her she's incredible. That she's energizing, engaging, vulnerable, funny, kind, and the only woman I want. That she makes me want to be the kind of guy who deserves her, a guy who can give her everything.

"I know, Nolan. It was foolish of me to kiss you like that," she says, suddenly cool, suddenly collected.

I blink, surprised, and correct her. "I kissed you."

"But I needed it," she says, stabbing her chest with her finger, annoyed with herself. "That was the problem. I needed it because I'm way too obsessed with the show and making it work, and it's making me do and say things, and you had to shut me up with a kiss. It's my fault."

"It's okay to *need* things. Or need a kiss," I say. Except, why am I arguing with her about kissing? That's not helpful.

"It's not okay," she says, building up a head of steam, and I want to defuse it for her. That's my instinct.

"Em, I'm sorry. I just . . ." I trail off because I don't have the tools to reassure her about this. "I just don't know what to say."

When she shutters her expression, I know those were the wrong words to speak. That's a break-up line, through and through. Because that's what I just did. I broke it off with her.

She stands, smooths her black shirt, grabs her backpack, and points to the door, and everything feels wrong.

Us ending feels wrong.

But if we don't end it, we miss our chance at the dreams we're chasing, barely catching.

She waves broadly to the street outside. "I have a quick call. My mom. She wanted me to call her. I'm going to do it in the room. I'll meet you in an hour at Break—"

I jump in. "Melt My Heart."

"Yes. That." Her answer sounds strangled. "The best grilled cheese in the . . ."

She doesn't finish. Maybe she can't. She just purses her lips and leaves.

Everyone is leaving.

Everything is a mess.

Most of all, my dumb heart, because I think I just broke up with the woman I'm madly in love with.

23

DOING IT AGAIN

Emerson

It seems wrong to indulge in such grilled cheese decadence today.

As I bite into the gooey, oozy Gouda, its deliciousness is a slap in the face.

How can anything taste good after I've been dumped?

The crowd gathers around our table. We've got quite an audience for this episode. I chew seductively, then lick the corner of my lips.

Someone calls out, "Give it that killer groan."

I do as they ask, with a long purr of praise. "So good."

Nolan grins at me, flirt in his eyes, a clever tilt to his lips. He seems barely affected by our split this morning.

But then, I doubt the break-up rule book has a

proviso for this twisted situation—*act turned on by the food you sample with the man who dumped you.*

Evidently, I'm a damn good actor because, as I ham it up, giving the fans the full foodgasm, no one seems to have a clue that, a little while ago, the man across from me scooped out my heart with a serrated melon ball spoon.

"So, Em. What's the verdict?" Nolan asks, setting me up with my catchphrase. "Would you *do it again*?"

His question pounds through my head. *Would* I do it again?

Kiss him again in Vegas? Sleep with him that night? Do it again in New York, then wander through the city with him, sharing my hopes and dreams?

Earlier memories fight their way to the front of my mind too. The night in college when we rearranged our friends' dorm. The day he agreed to be my new banana. The night at Jason's place before we left San Francisco.

Would I do it again?

Take the parrot flight? Race around Vegas grabbing grub to bring to the gingham-clad friends who embraced us with open arms? Slug him when he dodged the *Just Juice* and the turmeric? Protect him when Evelyn asked him about Inés Delacroix? Let him see my sloppy, naked, anxious heart?

Maybe I would. Because every time my anxiety about the show spun higher, Nolan settled me.

I don't know.

But at least I could fake certainty for the cameras. "Yes, I totally would," I answer, in a smoky tone.

I fake it for the crowd too, as we stay after the

recording, pose for pictures, and act like everything is what it's always been. But it's not.

We feel irretrievably broken, and I hate that.

When the last woman in a line of fans glances from Nolan to me and back, then starts to speak, asking, "Are you guys—"

I cut her off at the knees. "Nope. We're not."

"Cool," she says, then wheels around and leaves.

She doesn't even ask him out. I turn to him, shrug. "Sorry. I thought she was going to ask you on a date. You probably wanted her to."

Nolan stares at me like I've lost my mind. "No, I didn't."

He leaves the joint first, waiting for me on the street as I zip up my backpack. Maybe he needs space from me. When I reach the sidewalk, he gestures to it but says nothing as we walk to the hotel together.

We rarely walk in silence. But tonight, neither of us seems to have a word to say. And I don't like it. I don't like it at all.

When we reach the hotel, we find Max lounging in the lobby, flipping through a dog-eared copy of Jonathan Franzen's *The Corrections*. Because of course he reads Franzen. Rolling my eyes, I huff, ready to mutter to Nolan, *Franzen. Fucking Franzen.*

But I suck back the words. Can I still joke with him? Should I?

Nolan tips his head toward the sleek hotel bar where Marcos lifts a glass of red wine in an invitation. "I'm going to . . ."

"Go for it," I say, then I give a big yawn, selling my tiredness.

Nolan heads to the lobby bar, fist-bumping Marcos, and I start toward the elevator banks.

I steal a final glance at Max as I go by and see him smirking above his book. I don't know when or how he'll use his ammo about us. I'm not sure it matters—he kind of already pulled the trigger since the damage has been done.

As I reach my room, an email from Hayes flashes on my phone. With dread coiling in my gut, I click it open.

Hey, hey! Ilene emailed to say we should expect a decision in two more days. Chin up!

Weariness cloaks me as I wash off my makeup and get in bed. I text Katie to say hello, and we chat for a bit, catching up on everything, including my heartbreak. I spill the details, then ask—

Emerson: What do I do now?

Katie: You keep going.

Emerson: Like you did when it happened to you.

Katie: Yep. I'll always be here for you. I love you, friend. Know that.

Emerson: Love you too.

. . .

I run a finger over the screen. It's not nothing, having friends like this.

Hell, it's . . . everything.

Katie will still be around on the other side of two more days. So will Jo. So will my parents.

I hope Nolan will too.

* * *

The next morning, Nolan and I hit up a trendy vegan café for breakfast, then edit the hell out of the footage quickly for our YouTube channel.

I show him the final, and he says, "Looks good," then checks the time on his phone. "I'm going to meet the guys to work out."

"Cool. Hope you . . . lift lots of weights," I say, slapping on a stupid grin.

He laughs for a fraction of a second, but he doesn't get up, just drums his fingers on the table. "Have you thought about what you want to do when we've finished shooting?"

He says it so easily, like there's nothing we're waiting for—no verdict, no judgment.

I wish I had some of his calm. "Nope."

"Yeah. Me neither," he says. He stands to go but stops, curls a hand around my shoulder, then squeezes it hard.

Once he's gone, I let out a breath of relief.

Being with him hurts. Friendship-land doesn't feel so friendly at all. It's strained and awkward—a genie trying to stuff herself back into the damned lamp.

I exit the café too, drop my backpack at the hotel, then head to Central Park. Wandering over Gapstow Bridge, I stop to stare at the pond below, then I walk along the mall, drinking in the sights, the trees, the dogs, the kids, the people.

Briefly, I slip back in time to my road trip with Callie, our Route 66 tour that took us through Texas, around the Grand Canyon, into Nevada. We crossed the expansive United States, stopped at roadside diners and Cadillacs parked like popsicles on the side of the road. I flick through those pictures in my mind like a photo album, reliving the times we had.

I remember, too, the way she said, *thanks, babes,* when we cruised back into San Francisco, spent, exhausted, butts sore, but hearts full.

"You're welcome, babes," I said back.

Callie was never a New York fan. Part of me wishes she could see it through my eyes—the colors, the people, the bikers, the trails.

All the New Yorkness of it.

But that's okay. We wanted different things.

Like . . .

"Cutie pie!"

My gaze jerks to the warm, grandmotherly voice of Dot.

She wheels over to me on hot pink rollerblades, decked out in pink shorts, a gray sweatshirt, knee and elbow pads, and a matching helmet. Bette is by her side, dressed in red.

I glance around, then cup my mouth. "Where's your pit bull?"

Dot laughs and shushes me, holding a finger to her lips. "We escaped. Don't tell her."

"Evelyn doesn't want you to rollerblade?" I ask.

"She just wants us to be safe," Bette says.

"But sometimes we like to play." Dot shrugs. "We've always wanted to rollerblade. So, we're doing it."

"Just for fun," Bette adds.

That's the best reason ever. "Good for you."

Bette looks me up and down. "Why doesn't your smile reach your eyes, sweetie?"

I sigh. "Is it that obvious?"

Dot chimes in, "You look a little bit broken."

Called it. "Maybe I am."

"You ought to fix that, then. Maybe try rollerblading with us," Dot suggests.

That sounds like a brilliant idea, so I find the rental kiosk, change out of my shoes and into blades, then spend the afternoon chasing Dot and Bette around the park.

Afterward, they invite me to dinner, and over our meal of penne pasta at an Italian restaurant on Seventy-Second and Amsterdam, we don't talk about men, or work, or jobs.

In fact, I don't talk much at all.

Instead, I ask questions, listening to stories of their friendship, how they've known each other since kindergarten, how they depend on each other. How lucky they are to have this life.

I run my thumb over my ladybug charm.

I want *that*.

Not their life. But certainty in how to live my life.

I might not have the best friend I imagined I'd have for all my days, but I do know where I want to be. I do know what I want to do. Seeing these two women living their best life confirms what I've suspected for a while.

After I say goodnight to Dot and Bette, I call Jo and make plans to meet before she leaves tomorrow.

Then I make a harder call, this time to my mother. I have a question for her, and though I think I know the answer, I need *hers.*

So, I ask, and then I listen.

"Yes," she says after a thoughtful pause. "I do think that's what you've done." Her voice is a warm blanket wrapping around me as she speaks. "But maybe it's time to let that go?"

The thought panics me slightly. But yet, letting go is exactly what I need to do. What I started to realize that day in the park when Nolan and I talked about my terrible taste in men.

I may not have picked the best guys, but that isn't what's held me back. Something else has, and it's finally time to say goodbye to the one last reason I haven't let myself love.

24

RENT AND OTHER TRIFLING THINGS

Nolan

In the morning, my phone flashes with a text from Emerson.

Can you grab a cup of coffee with me before we say goodbye to Jo? There's something I want to talk to you about. Yes, I know that sounds ominous, but I promise it's not bad news.

No, what's bad news is she's inviting me for coffee and not to her room.

But that's on me. I'm the one who shut the door on us.

Thirty minutes later, I push open the door to Doctor Insomnia's Tea and Coffee Emporium, finding her waiting at a table with two cups of espresso. She looks radiant, and I want to kiss her eyelids, her cheek, her lips.

Instead, I sit across from her.

She slides a cup to me.

She's smiling. I half expect her to say *peace offering*.

I don't at all expect her to say what comes out of her mouth. "I want to stay in New York. No matter what happens with Webflix. I want to live here. So, I asked Jo to sublease her place to me," she says, takes a shuddery breath, then adds, "And she said yes."

"Wow. I didn't see that coming."

"Is that okay?" she asks nervously. "For the show. *How to Eat a Banana*. I won't do it if you think you can't make it work. But I want to try living here, and if you have to go back to San Francisco, we can do episodes remotely. We can do the kind where I try a restaurant in one city, and you do something similar in another, and we can still put out fun videos. We did that when you were in New York earlier this year," she says, her words spilling out.

"Right, our Zoom approach." I sound robotic. I don't know what else to say. I don't know how to feel except a little shitty.

Or shittier.

"Is that okay?" Emerson presses. "I just love it here. And I can't entirely afford Jo's rent, but she cut me a deal since her company in London is paying her housing for three months. So, she said she didn't need the full rate. And we've made some money with Webflix, of course, so I figure maybe in three months, I'll have paid off the loan, and I can snag some makeup jobs to help supplement the rent. I'm sure there are some good ones in New York."

That stings, and I know why. "You don't think our show will make it?"

"On Webflix?"

"Yes, Emerson. That one."

"Nolan," she says as if holding her ground. "You know I want it to, but I also want to start living my life."

"You don't think you were before?"

Her gaze is steady. She doesn't waver as she answers. "I think I was a little stuck in San Francisco. I was living in the apartment where I lived with my sister, driving her car, looking at photos of our last trip all the time. Now I'm here, and I feel like . . . like I can breathe."

This is the first time she's talked about her sister without sounding like she's gritting her teeth or teetering on the edge of anxiety. "I think it's awesome, then," I say, meaning it.

It's fantastic for her, and if I feel a little left behind, that isn't important. I've got to get over myself.

Emerson's my friend. She's always been my friend, and I need to win her back as a friend. "I think this is great."

"Do you?"

"I do." I down the espresso then roll up my sleeves. "Let's make a New York plan. And maybe even a to-do list."

"I love planning," she says with a sheepish grin.

"I know you do," I say.

"And I love to-do lists."

"I know that too." And even though we're close, so close I think I could map her mind and her heart, there's still so much more I want to know about her.

* * *

Goodbyes aren't new for me, so they should be easy. Since, well, it's what I do. I flit across the country, crashing here in New York, then there in San Francisco.

But saying goodbye to Jo thirty minutes later is neither hard nor easy. It's just weird. Since once we put her in the sleek town car that'll whisk her to the airport, I wish I could just walk away with Emerson, drape an arm around her shoulder, and kiss her cheek.

Talk about her plans.

Make more plans.

Instead, Emerson tosses Jo's keys in her palm, then tips her forehead to the cute building on West Seventy-Third Street. "I guess I'll check out my new pad."

TJ arches a brow, and Emerson quickly explains she'll be sticking around. He high-fives her. "Excellent. Let's get drinks next weekend then. But no musicals. I am not going to be your new musical buddy."

"Your deep disdain for musicals is well noted," she says.

When Easton takes off too, it's just TJ and me on an Upper West Side block, and my friend stares at me pointedly. "Soooo."

"So what?"

He rolls his dark eyes. "Dude."

The word contains multitudes.

"Okay, what's going on?" I ask, unsure what he's getting at.

He scoffs. "I think the question is, what's going on with you?"

Ah, well. There's no point pretending. TJ's astute, and I'm . . . well, I'm in need of some help. "Where do I even start?" I ask, a little lost. I wish I knew what to do with my desire to make plans with Emerson.

He claps my shoulder. "How about at the beginning?"

And so, as we walk away from Emerson, heading south along Central Park, I tell him. "I'm in love with Emerson, but I don't know how to make it work because of the show and Max, and Webflix, and her sister, and all those things."

"Those aren't little things, my friend."

"Yeah. They're big things, right?" I sigh heavily. So many damn obstacles.

He laughs. "They aren't big things either, buddy."

I whip my gaze to him. "They're only our career, my livelihood, some dickhead competitor, Emerson's issues with grief, and, ya know, all my shit too."

"But those aren't impediments."

"What do you mean?"

"You're in love with her. None of that matters," he says matter-of-factly.

I arch a skeptical brow. "None of them?"

TJ laughs. "Is that a question or a statement?"

That's all it takes, and his certainty becomes my own. The clarity of his understanding belongs to me now too. Those details don't matter. They are roadblocks, and I'll find a way around them because I want what's on the other side.

So, fuck everything else.

"It was a question. But it's a statement now," I say emphatically.

TJ blows out a breath like a proud teacher. "It's a good day when a man realizes what he wants."

We walk past a bank, where a screen flickers in the corner of the ATM lobby, streaming a news channel. The ticker tape below the anchor reads: *Jude Fox earns his first nomination.*

The picture switches to a good-looking blond dude flashing a winning grin as a reporter interviews him. I can't tell what he says, but he looks pleased.

TJ looks . . . stunned. And, also, he looks like he cares.

A lot.

"You know Jude Fox?"

He nods. "Yeah, I do."

"Jude Fox, as in the star of *If Found, Please Return*?"

"Yup."

I lift a brow, then realization dawns. "Ohhh. Is he why you went to Los Angeles that time you were all secretive about why you were going?"

With a heavy sigh, he nods. "Bingo. But that's a story for another time." He taps his watch. TJ doesn't need to tell me twice.

I know what I need to do.

Make big plans.

"The last time we went for a run. You said something about a friend," I say, prompting TJ.

"Yes. Yes, I did. The guy in Queens."

"Can I have his number?"

"I'll text it to you."

I take off, picking up the pace. Along the way, I call my brother and make plans that scare the hell out of me. Then I call Hayes, since my agent also happens to be my buddy, and I tell him about my big gamble. I'd tell him in person, but he's across the country at a movie premiere.

"Go for it. I'm behind you," Hayes says, and his support helps me keep moving forward with my decision, since TJ was right—all those things aren't hurdles.

Then, I text the guy in Queens. And when it's nearly time for Emerson and me to meet at the hotel with the network, I call her.

25

OTHER PLANS

Emerson

Jo's one-bedroom apartment—now mine for a spell—smells like lilacs. As I leave for the meeting at the hotel, locking the door behind me, I text Jo to tell her as much. She's taxiing on the JFK tarmac, ready to fly away on her new adventure.

Good luck on the other side of the ocean, I tell her.

Her reply is swift. *I hope you have your own fabulous adventure in New York.*

I hope so too.

I've needed a place that's all mine. That doesn't belong to my sister or my past. Something I can make my own.

There's only one thing I want all for myself. And thanks to the call with my mom and my decision to stay, I'm ready for it.

As I make my way back to the hotel, I start to dial Nolan to ask if he can meet before we see Ilene, but before I can tap in his name, it's flashing on the screen as the phone buzzes.

He hardly ever calls me. He usually texts. My heart scampers in my chest, maybe even cartwheels.

Luck. This feels like my ladybug luck.

I hope so deeply he wants the same thing I do, so fervently, that when I answer on half a ring, I know my voice is full of all my wishes.

"Hi," I say, a little breathless.

"Would you want to go on a date with me tonight? There's this great new restaurant I heard about, and I thought . . . No cameras. Just you and me. A date. In case that wasn't clear. A date."

I stop on the sidewalk. A block ahead of me, I spot the broad shoulders, the sly grin, the adorable glasses of my best guy friend. He's headed my way, cradling his phone to his face, and his smile is just for me.

For *phone* me, because he hasn't seen me yet.

"I'll tell you in person in about a block," I say, then I watch him scan the street until he finds me. With a grin, he ends the call and quickens his stride until he's standing in front of me.

He grabs my shoulders. "I don't care if we get the show. I don't care what happens with Webflix. I don't care if I have to crash with a friend or ask my brother for help with the loan. I don't care. I'm staying in New York because you're here and I want to be with you. And that's what I care about most. I'm in love with you, and I want to kiss you, again and again, every single day."

My heart sails away into the sky.

There are so many things to say to him. But sometimes you have to start a meal with dessert. So, I grab his face and kiss him.

It's better than the last time.

Better than the first time.

I seal my lips to his, my hand wrapping around his head, my fingers teasing into his hair, and laughter and joy bubbling on my tongue.

This kiss tastes like everything I was working for all along.

It's my hopes and dreams come true.

It's my big break.

I want this kiss more than I want anything else in the world. His lips are sweet, and he feels like part of my new life in New York.

One of the best parts.

When I break the kiss, I'm dizzy. "I love you," I say.

Nolan smiles, and I want to remember that smile forever. "I love you, honey," he says.

Tingles shoot down my spine. "I love it when you call me that."

"I know you do," he says, then presses his forehead to mine. "I'm sorry I ended things the other day. I've done some foolish things, but that takes the cake. I couldn't stop thinking how silly it was."

I shake my head. "You were trying to protect us. I get it."

"I was, but I don't want to lose you, no matter what Max says or doesn't say, and no matter what. Just no matter what."

I inch away, still riding this adrenaline high. "What changed your mind?"

"You," he says.

My brow creases. "What do you mean?"

"The way you decided you were staying. You're so fearless. So bold. And I knew I was going about everything the wrong way. I needed to say *fuck it* to all my fears too and grab hold of the thing—the person—I want most. *You.*"

I want to pinch myself to make sure this moment is real. "I want you, and I love you, and I want to do *How to Eat a Banana* with you in whatever form, but mostly, I want you to know this," I say, pursing my lips, trying to fight against the knot that's formed in my throat.

"What is it?" he asks as he strokes my hair.

I lift my chin, resolute. "I thought I had terrible taste in men because I was waiting for you, but that's not it," I say softly—but strong too.

He nods knowingly. "It's something else, isn't it?"

"You know why?"

"I think I do. But I want to hear it from you."

"I was afraid to fall in love because Callie wasn't going to," I say, and it's like slicing my skin open, revealing this hurt, exposing my guilt.

But it also feels like a new start.

Like fresh air on my skin. "I was afraid to have love because she wasn't going to," I say, my voice trembling.

He slides his fingers through my hair. "I had a feeling that's what was going on. So, what changed?"

"It started with rollerblading."

He laughs. "Okay, fill me in."

"I went with Dot and Bette, and that's when everything sort of hit me. I'd been hanging on to the pieces of my sister. And I knew I'd been afraid to have all the good things. Like love. This kind of love, big and powerful and terrifying and life-affirming."

He can't seem to rein in a grin at my description. "Did you realize she'd want you to?"

"No. I realized *I* want to. I want to have it," I say, squaring my shoulders.

His smile warms my soul. "Even better answer. And I want you to have all the good things. Including me."

"You're very, very good to me."

"I am. And I will be," he says. "I might not be great at a lot of things, but I'm really good at being your boyfriend. I plan to be the best at that. If you'll let me."

"Hmm," I say playfully. "I guess we'll find out at dinner."

"Oh, we're having more than dinner, honey."

"Does that mean you'll bend me over the bed and smack me later?"

"Obviously."

I kiss him a final time, then another, then once more before we go into the hotel. Right away, I spot Marcos and Drive-Thru Babe in the lobby, wrapped in a deep, big congratulatory embrace that tells me their collaboration got the slot.

I head over to them, refusing to feel jealous. I won't

let envy get the better of me. “Congrats,” I tell Marcos. “We’re so excited for you.”

“Yeah, congrats, man,” Nolan says.

“Thank you. I couldn’t be happier,” Marcos says.

Funny thing. Maybe we didn’t get the show, but I couldn’t be happier either.

26

HEALTH FOOD NO MORE

Nolan

We aren't scheduled to meet with Ilene for another fifteen minutes, so after extracting ourselves from the Marcos hug, I pull Emerson into the elevator, push her against the wall, and pin her hands to her sides.

Then I kiss her ruthlessly as we pass each floor on the way to my room. In a heartbeat, she's grinding against me, seeking out friction with my hard-on as I devour her lips.

I crush her mouth in the kind of cutthroat kiss that makes her gasp and sigh. Soon, the elevator reaches the twelfth floor, and the second we're in 1205, I unzip her jeans, and she does the same for me.

I rip off my glasses and find a condom while she wiggles out of her jeans. Then I'm covered, and I hike up her leg around my hip and sink inside.

She shudders, her whole body surrendering to the feel of us together as she ropes her arms around my neck. Looking up at me, she licks her lips. "Watch me. Look at me," she murmurs.

"Always," I groan as I thrust into her.

She clenches around my cock, and heat coils in my body.

This feels so right. So good.

It's only been days, but it feels like forever when you miss the person you love madly. "Missed you," I whisper.

"So much," she says, finishing the sentence.

Yes, it's the same for both of us.

I grip her hips, push deeper, fuck her harder, but I also give her something else she wants.

A kiss.

Only this time, I'm slow.

Teasing.

Barely brushing my lips over hers in a gentle, intimate kiss, telling her without words that we can fuck hard or slow, kiss rough or soft. We can have it all.

"Whatever you want, honey," I rasp out, "I'll give you."

"I know," she says, panting. "I know."

That feels like a brand-new promise too—that I'll give her what she needs in and out of bed.

Soon, though, the thinking subsides, and we're reduced to noises.

The slap of skin.

The feel of warm bodies.

Until she comes on a breathless gasp, and I follow her there, losing my mind.

Then, we slow down until I still and brush my lips to her neck, the spot of her bruise. It's still a little tender, a little blue.

"Love your mark," I whisper. "Love you."

"Love you so much."

A few minutes later, we're in the bathroom, straightening up for our meeting, and she catches my eye in the mirror. "What did you mean about the loan? And asking your brother for help? I was a little preoccupied with kissing your face, so I didn't quite get everything."

I hold her gaze as I put on my clothes. "I called and asked him to float me the rest of the money for Inés's loan. I don't want him to pay it off for me; I just need an advance. I'm going to look for work as a line cook somewhere in the city to help make my rent. TJ has a friend in Queens who's subleasing, so I figure with our YouTube money and some line-cook dough, I'll be able to cover the bills and pay him back for the final loan payments. I decided to just get over it—my need to do it all on my own. He likes to help, so he's happy to get the debt off the books. And I want to be here in New York."

Emerson dips her face, looking a little sheepish. "That's so sexy."

I laugh. "It's sexy, me asking for help from my little brother?"

She nods then meets my gaze. "Yeah. It totally is. You were pretty stubborn."

"Pot. Kettle."

"That's why I recognize it. And I'm impressed. I know that wasn't easy," she says.

"It was worth it to be with you," I say.

Fourteen minutes after making out in the elevator, we head downstairs, ready to meet the pink-haired whirling dervish. "I bet she takes us to a quinoa joint," I say.

"An acai berry one," Emerson suggests.

"An acai berry, chia seed, quinoa, and kale shop," I say, not to be outdone.

When we reach the lobby, I'm surprised to recognize two ladies I adore, hugging in front of reception. Evelyn is there too, embracing both of them as all three bounce in excitement.

Hmmm. That's interesting, and I'm not sure what to make of their moment.

So I focus on my mission. At the edge of the lobby, I find Ilene by her shock of pink hair. She paces, talking on the phone, and when she sees us, she waves us over then gestures for us to follow her out of the hotel.

We do, and the whole time we're walking down the street, she keeps up the *uh-huhs* and *yups* and *got its*.

Until we reach a kombucha shop, where Ilene stops as she ends her call, and stuffs her phone into her purse. "That's done, so now we can get a little something," Ilene says.

Emerson looks from the door to Ilene. "I had a coffee, but Nolan would love any type of kombucha." Then my girlfriend winks at me, mouthing *sucker*.

"I'm going to make you pay for that," I whisper.

But Ilene just laughs. "Please. I have someplace else in mind."

All I can think is *thank fuck,* since I hate kombucha.

She ushers us a few doors down to a lunch spot called The Happy Cow. A quick scan of the menu tells me it's vegetarian. A quick scan of my memory bank reminds me it's the first place Emerson and I reviewed together—the one in San Francisco, that is.

"Want lunch? This place has great salads, sandwiches, veggie burgers. You name it." Ilene smiles at me unapologetically. "I'm a vegetarian too, so I thought it'd be perf. Hope you don't mind. And I am soooo hungry I could eat a whole plant."

The woman is a hoot. "I'm an equal opportunity eater," I say.

"And I love veggie sandwiches," Emerson puts in.

Ilene flashes her a knowing grin then winks. "I know. I've watched every single episode of your show."

When we've placed our orders, I wait for Ilene to ask for a charcoal shake, or a hemp seed smoothie, or a grass platter. Instead, she reaches for a glass of ice water, drops a straw in it, and drinks, then sighs happily. "So, how's it going?"

"Great," I say, wondering when she's going to get around to letting us down easy.

Ilene looks to Emerson. "And you? You look hawt, Emerson. Your cheeks are all rosy red."

Emerson swallows, maybe a little embarrassed. Or maybe not, since she reaches for my hand and threads her fingers through mine. "I feel fabulous."

Ilene's eyebrows climb, and her lips twitch, but she says nothing.

"We're together," Emerson adds, and there's that big mouth on my woman.

I love her big mouth.

"Yes, we are," I add. "We just wanted you to know. Not that it matters now, per se. But we wanted you to know from us."

Take that, Max.

"And we know that Marcos got the slot. He's really talented. You made a great choice," I add.

But then, back in the hotel, Dot and Bette seemed stoked too. I'm not sure what to make of that.

"Marcos is incredible," Ilene agrees. "So are Dot and Bette."

She sips her water then sets it down again. "That's why I hired them for our new food sub-channel. We had such success with all the food shows that we're launching an entire sub-channel devoted to cuisine. Let's be honest—people love to eat."

Well, yeah. It makes life and stuff possible. "That they do," I agree.

"And that's why we want your show to be the lead show on Webflix itself, to attract new viewers and then bring them to the sub-channel. Sort of the marquee property among our food shows. It'll have top placement, and we'll promote it . . ."

She keeps talking, but I can't process the details because I just shot into the stratosphere on a Webflix-fueled rocket.

This is so much more than I ever expected, and it feels surreal.

When Ilene's done, she says, "So what do you think?"

Emerson turns to me, her green eyes shining, her hand gripping mine, and then everything feels fantastically, terrifically real.

And worth every single bump in the road.

I lean into Emerson, forehead to forehead, and just breathe in the moment. The joy of this news. The thrill of creating something from nothing, building it from the ground up, pouring love, sweat, work, tears, late nights, and wild hopes into it.

For a chance.

When we break apart, Emerson takes off, firing off questions a million miles a minute, and I just sit back and watch my girlfriend, my best friend, my partner steer our ship toward a whole new future.

Yes, every single day was worth it.

Not because of the show, but because of the woman by my side. The person I get to work with. The person I get to love.

27

ON A SCALE OF ONE TO TEN

Emerson

Ordinarily, I don't like hot dogs. Which is weird, since, hello? Phallic food is fun. But hot dogs I can take or leave.

Usually, leave.

That was before I found Your Dog Loves These Wieners, a food truck in Central Park with dachshund drawings all over the vehicle and decadent veggie dogs on the menu.

I lift the long dog, bring it to my mouth, and meet Nolan's eyes. "Will it fit?"

With a snort, he turns to the camera, delivers an aside. "She said the same thing to me last night."

I roll my eyes. *This guy*. "Please. I'm the mistress of handling *that*. I'm talking about this veggie dog, babe."

"Try it, *honey*."

"I will," I say, then open wide and bite down. And wow. Just holy delicious fake meat, that tastes fantastic mixed with mustard and avocados and pesto and happiness.

I moan around the dog.

"Damn, that's quite a foodgasm," he remarks.

"But would you do it again?" a voice calls out from the crowd gathered around the truck.

I meet the young woman's bright blue eyes, glance at her inked arms, her excited smile. The question echoes through my mind like it did at the vegan café a few months ago when I was missing Nolan dreadfully. When I was trying to figure out all my stuff. What I'd fight for. What I'd ask for. What I could let go of. What I desperately wanted to have.

Now, the question's easy to answer.

I'd do it all again, every second, because I love where I am. I'm living my best life, not Callie's or anyone else's.

So, the answer is *yes.*

Though, right now, the inked fan only wants to know if I'd do the dog again. And that answer is an easy one too.

"Yes. This one's a ten."

Nolan pretends to stumble. "Whoa. You've never given a ten before."

He's right. I give good scores, but never perfect ones.

I shrug. "This hot dog rates it. There's just one other thing I'd give a ten."

"What's that?" he asks.

I step forward, drop a chaste kiss onto his lips, then say, "You."

The audience coos.

He blushes.

And I swoon like I do every day with my co-host—my love.

Nolan's my ten, and maybe that's why our show turned into a bona fide hit. We've always had chemistry. Turns out that was more powerful than all the what-ifs in the world.

After the shoot, we head up Central Park West to our place. Nolan never got the sublease in Queens. He moved into Jo's apartment with me. It made financial sense and all the other kinds of sense too. I want to be with him. He wants to be with me.

So, we're together.

It was that simple.

It *just* was.

And I breathe, free and easy, at last.

Other things are simple too. Like friendships—a few nights later, Katie and Harlan fly into town for a sports award gala. Jason is here too, heading to a related event—a pro-athlete player auction.

"Bet you only go for a dollar tomorrow," Nolan ribs when Jason joins us at Gin Joint.

"More like top dollar," Jason says. He ruffles Nolan's hair then brings me in for a big hug. "Thank you for making my brother happy," he whispers.

I hug him harder. "It goes both ways."

"I know. He only talks about you all the time. And

always has." He lets go just as Katie and Harlan push through the bar's front door.

Jason flops onto the couch, tipping his chin toward Nolan. "As for tomorrow night's auction, I've got my best suit. No one can resist a hot athlete in a sharp suit."

Katie jumps right into the conversational fray. "Suits are catnip. They're pretty much the reason I stay with this clown," she says, pointing to her hubs.

Harlan clears his throat then pats Katie's growing belly. "My suits and my offspring, sweetheart."

Katie plants a kiss on his cheek. "That too."

A little later, Jo sails into Gin Joint, looking fabulous, practically glowing. I squeal when I see her, then race over and give her a hug. "Details. Tell me everything about London and *that guy*," I say.

She's kept me updated about her life and love overseas via FaceTime and texts, but I steal her for a few minutes and get the latest.

"So, there you go," she says when she's done.

"I can't wait to find out what happens next," I say.

With a laugh, she admits, "Me too."

When we rejoin the group, Nolan's chatting with Katie and Harlan, so I turn to Jason, eager to hear what my boyfriend's brother is up to. The auction is a big deal to him, and I have a feeling all his suit-wearing plans are deliberate.

"So is there someone in particular you hope won't resist you in your suit?"

With a smile, he dips his face. And yes, I think it's safe to say he's hoping something —or someone— happens at the auction.

EPILOGUE

THE LUCKY GUY

Jason

That is an excellent question.

With a very complicated answer.

Is there a guy I hope shows up? Yes. But will he bid on me, or expect me to bid on him?

No idea.

I still don't know what Beck wants from me or what I want from him, even after the night he banged on the door at my place and told me the truth about what happened a year ago.

That night he confessed to a lot of things that surprised the hell out of me.

And, admittedly, excited me too.

But a few weeks later, I'm still trying to figure out the other starting quarterback in San Francisco. Like I said, it's complicated.

"There might be someone in particular," I tell Emerson.

She nudges my arm. "Who's the lucky guy?"

I lean closer, whisper in her ear. "I promise to tell you. . .when I figure it all out."

"You better figure it out soon. I want to know!"

"Of course you do," I say, then add with a sigh, "And so do I."

"Well, I hope that happens sooner rather than later," she says.

And she's not the only one who wants to know what's up in my love life, since when my friend TJ joins us at Gin Joint a little later, he proceeds to grill me about the auction. "So, what's the verdict? Have you decided?"

If only this were as easy as knowing who to throw to on the football field. "On a suit, yes. On a plan, no."

TJ chuckles. "So, basically you have no fucking clue what you'll do if Beck bids on you tomorrow?"

"It's pretty much going to be a line of scrimmage decision. But hey, feel free to attend tomorrow and find out who bids on who."

"Maybe I will," TJ says, then my brother tears his attention away from Emerson and Jo, and back to me.

"I could offer a cooking metaphor for you, Jaybird. Like, maybe you need to let this romantic situation marinate a little longer," Nolan says.

"Or he could take it off the heat," TJ offers.

I grin, maybe a little wickedly. "I do like the heat though," I say.

That's another reason why I'd really like to figure

out what Beck wants from me, and what I want from him. But for now, I focus on my brother, and all our friends.

EPILOGUE

FRIENDSHIP GOALS

Nolan

This is better than shishito peppers.

An evening here in my new city with friends and family, and New York is right where I belong.

Especially as I watch my little brother and my good friend rib each other. When TJ teases Jason about Beck, my brother's blue eyes go a little dreamy.

I could tease Jason, but I know there's more to it for him. Maybe there has been for some time. Just like there was for me. Like there seems to be for TJ and Jude. And like there seems to be for Jo as she catches us all up to speed on her new romance in London.

As I look around my circle of friends, soaking in the moment, I suppose we're all like that—here for each other through ups and downs, stops and starts, pain and heartbreak.

And all the joy, too, on the other side.

I found mine with Emerson, and I've got new dreams for the two of us. As Jo and Em chat, as Jason and TJ strategize, and as Katie and Harlan talk and laugh, I drape an arm around my best friend, my co-creator, my girlfriend.

My. . .everything.

Emerson snuggles close to me as everyone reconnects, and drops a quick kiss to my cheek. "Love you, friend," she says.

"Love you too, friend," I say, and enjoy the rest of the night here with them, then later, alone with her.

EPILOGUE

A VERY NAKED PARROT

Emerson

The parrot squawks. "So, a parrot walks into a bar . . . and he's naked."

I turn to Nolan, mouthing, *Aren't parrots always naked*?

Nolan nods the answer. *Yes.*

"And he says to the bartender, the two of us will have a couple of blow jobs," the bird continues.

I tug on Nolan's shirt, whisper in his ear, "That's a very dirty parrot."

"Yes, he might even be dirtier than you."

I scoff. "I wouldn't go that far."

The emerald-green bird squawks once more. "And the bartender says *a couple of blow jobs?* There's only one of you."

The bird drops his beak like he's looking at his

birthday suit-ed body. "It's for me and my . . . woodpecker."

I groan—so loudly—and roll my eyes. But I'm laughing, and so is Nolan, and we keep on laughing through the whole set of terrible jokes at The Parrot Club.

After the show, we catch a cab to our hotel. "We finally made it to The Parrot Club," I say as the driver pulls away from the curb.

"My life is now complete," Nolan says. "I can't think of anything else I want to do."

"You don't want to ride the roller coaster?"

"Ah, yes. That. Let's do that."

I have high hopes for the ride.

We tell the driver to stop at New York, New York, and we wind our way through the casino to the thrill ride where we had our first kiss. It feels a little like kismet, like something big could happen. I can't stop thinking both of beginnings and next steps. Of the future I want with Nolan.

As we wait in line, I squeeze his hand. "You're the reason I love roller coasters."

"You're the reason I'm ridiculously happy, so I win," he says with a cheeky grin. Then he stows his glasses in the locker, and we grab seats in the car.

On the first hill, I maybe, possibly, definitely squeeze his arm hard enough to leave marks. But there's always makeup to cover that. When we zip downhill, though, I thrust my arms into the air and scream at the top of my lungs.

It's more fun than the first time.

Everything with Nolan is, including this mini vacation in Vegas. Our show is going strong, and Webflix renewed it for another season, along with Dot and Bette's and the Wine Dude and Drive-Thru-Babe's too. Not Max's. I don't feel bad about that at all. Not one bit.

Nolan and I decided to celebrate by flying to Vegas. He played solitaire on the flight, and I read.

My goal in Vegas? Do face masks and wear robes. Translation—we bang a lot, just like we do back home in New York. But hey, every couple has hobbies. Ours are food and sex.

When we're off the ride, Nolan kisses me like he did that very first time. It's toe-tingling and knee-weakening, and I could kiss him all night. But kisses end, and this glorious one does too. Nolan grabs his glasses, and we leave. Once we're out of New York, New York, I'm still a little surprised that he didn't ask me a certain question. But I'm not disappointed.

I can wait. I can definitely wait.

Good things come and all.

We return to The Extravagant, and as we wander through the hotel on the way to the elevators, I figure tonight's not the night, and that's okay.

"Hey!" Nolan points to a late-night eatery off the casino. "I didn't realize they had a cereal bar here."

I'm Pavlov's dog. Instantly, my mouth waters. "Cinnamon Life Cereal, take me to your leader."

Nolan pats my belly. "Your appetite for cereal knows no bounds."

"That is true. It is boundless."

With an arm wrapped around my shoulder, he guides me into the quirky breakfast-anytime café.

We grab stools at the bar and place our order with the server. "One bowl of Froot Loops for me."

"One Cinnamon Life Cereal for me," I add.

A minute later, the server returns with a bowl for him and a box for me. "I don't need a whole box, but thank you," I say.

The server shrugs and smiles. "Here you go anyway."

Then he walks away.

I arch a brow at Nolan, who's pouring a cup of milk onto his multi-colored cereal. "Am I supposed to open the box?"

"That's how one gets to the cereal inside," he says like he has a secret. "And the prize."

"Oh, there's a prize?" I ask, refusing to get ahead of myself.

I swear I try. But it's hard.

"Yes, there is," Nolan says.

I rip the box open and gasp so loud I bet they can hear me at New York, New York.

There's a blue velvet box perched on top of the cereal.

I grab it, hold it tight. Try not to burst into a million diamonds of excitement.

"Like I said." In that commanding way he sometimes has with me, Nolan takes the box, rises from the barstool, and gets down on one knee.

I have no chill.

"Oh my God," I whisper. It turns into a whisper-chant. "Oh my God, oh my God."

"Emerson Alva, you're the one. The one I want to wake up with, sleep with, work with, eat with, play with. You're the person I want to spend my days and nights with. And you're the person I want to spend the rest of my life with. Will you marry me?"

I jump off the stool, tears streaking down my face, and join him on the floor, throwing my arms around his neck.

"I will."

He slides the ring on my finger. "Good. Now shut up and kiss me," he says.

And I do—because that sounds like an excellent plan to me.

* * *

What happens to Jo when she heads to London? Find out in the ultra romantic, forbidden office romance **Kismet**! You can order it now! And read on for a preview!

Why was TJ so transfixed with the report about Jude? What happened during his weekend in Los Angeles? You'll learn all those delicious details when you fall hard for TJ and Jude's romance unfolds in **Hopelessly Bromantic**! Order now while this epic romance is on a preorder discount! I've got a sneak preview for you below!

Don't forget Jason! The sexy quarterback's story comes in THE BOYFRIEND COMEBACK and you'll discover what happened with Beck as Jason fights not to fall for his rival!

Be sure to sign up for my mailing list to be the first to know when swoony, sexy new romances are available or on sale!

Jo…

He gestures to my Hazel Valentine book. "Speaking of libraries and things to check out, are you enjoying your book?"

My face heats slightly, and I hesitate. When you tell a person what you read, sometimes their reaction reveals who they are. Some judge, and some don't. I prefer the latter. "It's a love story," I say, lifting my chin.

His expression goes serious. "Is it an escape?"

"You're not going to tease me about reading romance novels?" I ask.

His brow knits in confusion. "Is that a thing people do?"

So much. Too often. I've been ridiculed for my taste in books, my love of musicals, my affection for pop songs. "Some people think you should only read *serious literature* or *important non-fiction*."

Heath's expression is comically astonished. "People mock reading? Make fun of books? Well, besides silly quote books culled from social media feeds."

"Social media is fair game for mockery. And yes,

some people mock reading, and certain types of stories," I say with a laugh.

"People," he mutters, like he disapproves of them in general.

"I like people, generally. But now that I've said it, that does sound unbelievably petty of them."

He taps the back cover of my book gently. "How does the book make you feel?"

The question makes me dig into my emotions about the story, examine them, and I like that. I flip to the back cover, featuring a couple kissing on the streets of New York, and my heart glows a little. "Possible," I say. "It makes me feel . . . *possible*."

Discover Jo's romance Kismet!

And now here's a peek at the day TJ meets Jude in **Hopelessly Bromantic**! The price goes up on release day!

TJ...

When I wander down the little lane in Covent Garden, it's as if I've traveled to my personal paradise. Shops line the quaint alley full of books—my favorite things after sex and pizza.

I could get lost and never want to be found. Except I *do* want to find Jude. What are the chances he'll be in one of these shops *right now?*

Maybe it's best to focus on my original mission. Even before I left the States, I wanted to go to the bookshop I'd visited as a kid. No, not that one with the medical textbooks.

Definitely not the children's bookstore with the stuffed dragon in the window.

And for sure it's not the shop with globes in the window.

When I've scoured nearly the whole alley, I'm convinced the store I camped out in a decade ago has closed.

Until a sign beckons me.

An Open Book.

It feels like déjà vu.

Peering inside, I breathe a sigh of relief. This is the store. Jude is probably history, and soon, he'll be a hazy memory of my first day in London—just some cute guy I met one afternoon.

A bell tinkles as I enter. I don't see a shopkeeper. Maybe they're in the back?

I browse the shelves, checking out row after row of colorful spines, stories in each one that lure me to read and also to write. I reach a row of works by Oscar Wilde, one of the greatest Irish writers ever. That dude was funny as fuck.

As I tip a copy of *The Importance of Being Earnest* into my hand, the thump of a hardback tome rattles a shelf behind me and I jerk my head.

Then I turn.

And wow.

This must be kismet.

Jude's paused in the act of sorting books, surprised to see me, it seems. And he looks—impossibly—even better than he did a few hours ago.

"You found the shop," he says, his lips twitching with the hint of a grin, his blue eyes full of mischief.

All at once, everything feels a little heady and a lot possible. Like this is the start of something. My fingers tingle, and I'm not even sure why. But maybe it's just from this dizzying sense of . . . fate.

And fear.

I don't want to fuck this up. Life doesn't give you a lot of chances. So I don't answer him right away. "Well, I had a few clues," I finally say.

Maybe I was wrong. Maybe I *did* step off the plane and into my very own rom-com.

"It's good to be an amateur detective," he tosses back.

So that's how we're doing it—going toe to toe and quip to quip. Bring it on. "Who said anything about amateur?"

His lips curve into a sly grin. "Ohhh . . . you're a professional detective?"

"How else would I have found An Open Book?"

His eyes travel up and down my body. "Sheer determination."

I laugh. "Yes, a little bit of that, but someone left a few hints. It was like a scavenger hunt. Maybe that's my new calling—scavenger hunting."

"Didn't know that was a thing. You do learn something new every day," he says. Then he makes that wildly sexy move again as he did outside TK Maxx—he coasts his teeth over that lower lip. I stifle a groan. My God, does he know what that does to a man?

Who am I kidding? Of course he does. A guy who looks, talks, stands like that—he's gorgeous and knows it.

Hell, he makes leaning against a shelf sexy.

"You know what I learned today?" I ask, plucking at my new Tetris shirt. It's nice and snug and makes my chest look good.

"Dying to know."

"That Angie's Vintage Duds does, in fact, have good clothes. Appreciate the tip."

"Would I lead you astray?"

That's an excellent question. I glance down at *The Importance of Being Earnest* in my hand as I hunt for retorts, then I look up, our gazes locking. "I have no idea, Jude. Would you?"

He laughs easily. Bet he does everything easily. Pose, walk, talk, read, live.

"Not when it comes to important matters like finding just the right shirt, and just the right store, and just the right book." He steps closer, taps the Wilde I'm holding. If an electrical charge could jump through pages, it just did. My skin is sizzling, almost like he touched me rather than paper.

"Like this book. Is that what you came to the store for?" Jude asks it so damn innocently, like he's goading me into admitting I came here for him.

Of course, I did. But two can play at this flirting game. I waggle the book. "I just needed to brush up on my Wilde."

"Naturally. You're just here for the books," he says, calling me on my patent lie.

"It's a bookstore. Why else would I come?" I counter.

"There couldn't be *any* other reason," he says. "But I'd be a terrible shop assistant if I didn't help you find just the right Wilde." He takes his time with his speech so that each word can send a wicked charge through me.

They all do.

"Except, I don't even know your name," he adds.

I glance around. The shop is empty, except for a couple of young women parked on comfy chairs in the corner, flipping through guidebooks, maybe. They're wrapped up in their world. I hope they stay there for hours.

"I'm TJ," I say.

A laugh bursts from Jude.

"My name is funny to you?" I ask.

"That's so very American," he says.

"What do you know? I am American," I say. "And I know you don't do the whole initial thing here. Does that mean you prefer to be Jude the Third?"

Another laugh. "If I'd told you I was Jude the Third, I doubt you would've come looking for—" He sounds like he's about to say *me*, but he amends it, quickly shifting to, "All the Wildes. Besides, I'm just Jude."

But he's not just Jude.

He's not *just* at all.

I keep that thought locked up tight. "And if I'd told you what TJ stands for, you'd know exactly why some Americans prefer initials," I say.

His blue eyes sparkle with intrigue. "You have to tell me now, TJ." My name sounds like a bedroom whisper on his lips.

"You'll never get that out of me," I say, matching his breathless tone.

He arches a brow. "Never? Never ever, you say?"

I could dine on his charm. I could eat breakfast, lunch, and dinner on his wit. I never want to leave this store. We can play word badminton till after dark. I'll stop only when the lights go down, and we can do all the other things—the things I'm already picturing with that lush, red mouth of his.

"Never," I repeat, then take a long, lingering moment. "Unless you have your ways."

He hums, a rumbly sound low in his throat. Then he taps his chin. "Perhaps I could guess. Thomas James?"

I shake my head. "Not even close."

"Theodore John." He makes a rolling gesture. "I could go all night."

"I hope so. And, perhaps, you should," I say.

Over drinks. Over sex. Over breakfast.

But the shop bell tinkles.

Jude groans as a customer strolls in. "I have to go wait on a customer."

And I have to make sure you and I go out tonight.

But before I can say *You'll find me here by the Oscar Wildes,* Jude adds, "Don't go anywhere, Thiago Jonas."

"You're not even warm," I say as he walks past me, brushing his shoulder against mine.

"But I bet you are," he whispers.

I try to stifle the hitch in my breath. But it's hard

with this man, and his mouth, and his face, and my good fortune.

"Very," I say, low, just for him.

"Good," he says, then strides to the front of the store and chitchats with a customer. The whole time he ushers her around, my neck is warm, my head is hazy, and I feel like this is happening to some other guy. Like this is just a figment of my jet-lagged brain.

I flip open the book, turn it to one of my favorite scenes, and hear the lines in Jude's voice.

It's never sounded better.

A few minutes later, Jude returns, sliding up by my side to read over my shoulder, his breath near my ear. "*I hope you have not been leading a double life, pretending to be wicked and being good all the time. That would be hypocrisy.*" He stops before I melt, because yeah, that's the best I've ever heard this play. "Do you like Oscar Wilde?"

"Very much so," I say, trying to stay cool. "You?"

"A lot," he says, and neither one of us is talking about the Irish poet.

But I feel Wilde would approve of everything I'm about to do.

"Go out with me tonight, Jude," I say, as a tangle of heat rushes down my chest, curls into a knot in my belly.

"I was hoping you'd ask. *But* . . ." He pauses, and my stomach plummets. This is when he'll disappoint me. "I have to work till nine. Can you meet at nine-thirty?

That's it? That's the *but*? I would meet him at three in the morning. At noon. Now.

I keep all that eagerness to myself. "Yeah. Want to meet at a pub? Get a beer? That sounds so very English."

"And it also sounds so very good," he says. "Where are you staying?"

"Not far from here. My hotel's near Piccadilly Circus."

"Meet me at The Magpie."

"I'll be there."

He points to the book. "Is this the edition you came for? The one with the two men in top hats?"

"It's perfect."

"Did you really want the book?"

I swallow roughly, meet his eyes, speak the whole truth. "I really want the book," I say, and it's not a lie. It also might have a double meaning.

As he heads to the counter, I follow him. I feel like I'd follow him anywhere, and that's a dangerous thought. But now's not the time for analyzing.

Now is a time for doing.

Jude rings me up, slides the card reader across the counter, then takes out his phone. After I swipe my credit card, he says, "And I believe you were going to give me your number, TJ."

As I slide him the card reader, he gives me his phone. I keep my head down, so he can't see the size of my smile as I tap in my digits then swivel the device back to him. Seconds later, he sends me a text.

Jude: Mark my words. I'll figure out what TJ stands for. I have my ways.

. . .

TJ: Just try them on me.

Then, since it's always good to leave them wanting more, I take the Wilde and go. As I walk off, I can see the rest of my days and nights in London in a whole new way.

You can order Hopelessly Bromantic everywhere!

And now here's a preview of Jason's romance in THE BOYFRIEND COMEBACK ...

Jason...

He bends closer and hands me the cat, his fingers brushing mine.

He did not just touch me intentionally. That was a cat handoff, that's all.

As he heads away to the bathroom, I drag a hand through my hair, trying to process the shift in the mood —the date-like feel of the night, the way he's giving off flirty vibes.

But then, I press the brakes.

I don't know Beck from Adam. Don't know his

agenda, so it's best to assume it's truly just this TV show he's staying for.

"I'm getting the distinct impression you have a crush on my dog." The feminine voice from the TV show reconnects me to reality. Well, TV reality.

Shit. I didn't even pause the show when Beck left. The clicker's in the middle of the couch, so I scoot over and grab it, point it at the screen, and back up thirty seconds.

Beck returns to the living room, circling the couch. To get back to his seat, he has to go by me, and his dark eyes are on mine as he slinks past. "You stole my cat," he says, his tone teasing, flirty, his eyes sparkling.

What is going on?

He sits down.

Closer to me.

He's a whole cushion closer.

I don't know what to do.

"Anything good happen while I was gone?" he asks.

I swallow, trying to form words. "I rewound it," I say, stating the obvious since the screen is paused.

Then I hit play, and I do my damnedest to watch *Unfinished Business.* When Jamie and Zoe stop in the stairwell, I don't move. I laser in on the screen. The kiss gets a little hot, a little heavy.

No idea what Beck is doing, and I refuse to peek, even when Bandit leaves my lap to curl up in his.

Lucky cat.

When the episode ends, I bet he'll say thanks and take off. But once the credits roll, he clears his throat, takes a breath, then blurts out, "Want to watch another?"

His question is Mach speed as if it's fueled by hope.

A spark slides down my spine. I'm supposed to be in control. But I don't feel that way right now.

And I like that feeling too much.

"Sure."

THE BOYFRIEND COMEBACK is available everywhere!

Easton's romance is available in **COME AGAIN**, and Katie and Harlan's romance is told in **A Wild Card Kiss!**

ALSO BY LAUREN BLAKELY

FULL PACKAGE, the #1 New York Times Bestselling romantic comedy!

BIG ROCK, the hit New York Times Bestselling standalone romantic comedy!

THE SEXY ONE, a New York Times Bestselling standalone romance!

THE KNOCKED UP PLAN, a multi-week USA Today and Amazon Charts Bestselling standalone romance!

MOST VALUABLE PLAYBOY, a sexy multi-week USA Today Bestselling sports romance! And its companion sports romance, MOST LIKELY TO SCORE!

WANDERLUST, a USA Today Bestselling contemporary romance!

COME AS YOU ARE, a Wall Street Journal and multi-week USA Today Bestselling contemporary romance!

PART-TIME LOVER, a multi-week USA Today Bestselling contemporary romance!

UNBREAK MY HEART, an emotional second chance USA Today Bestselling contemporary romance!

BEST LAID PLANS, a sexy friends-to-lovers USA Today Bestselling romance!

The Heartbreakers! The USA Today and WSJ Bestselling rock star series of standalone!

P.S. IT'S ALWAYS BEEN YOU, a sweeping, second chance romance!

MY ONE WEEK HUSBAND, a sexy standalone romance!

CONTACT

You can find Lauren on Twitter at LaurenBlakely3, Instagram at LaurenBlakelyBooks, Facebook at LaurenBlakelyBooks, or online at LaurenBlakely.com. You can also email her at laurenblakelybooks@gmail.com

CPSIA information can be obtained
at www.ICGtesting.com
Printed in the USA
BVHW030204180322
631848BV00007B/19